AF352462

ROUTE 36

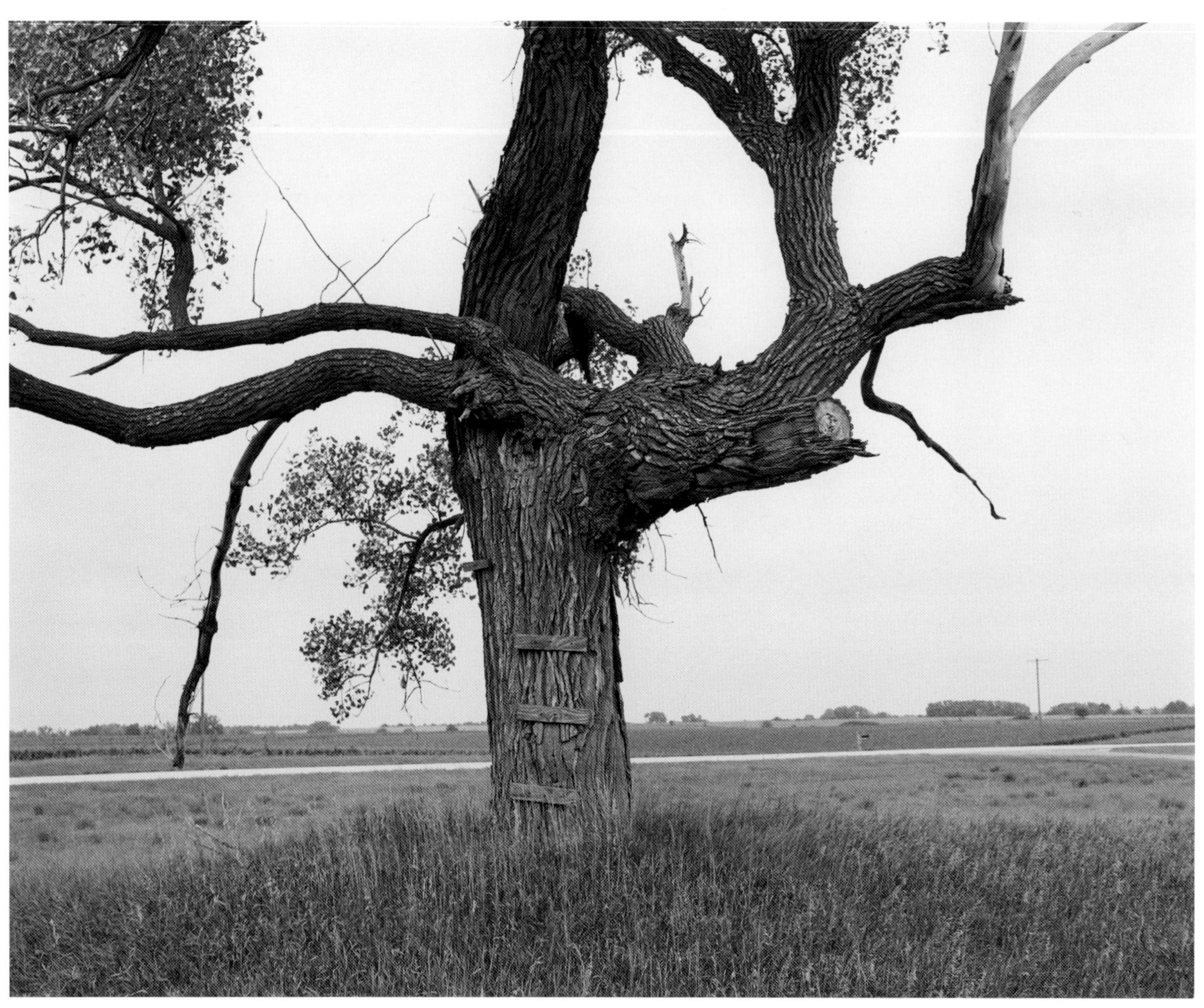

WILLIAM WYLIE

ROUTE 36

FOREWORD BY MERRILL GILFILLAN

FLOOD EDITIONS 2010

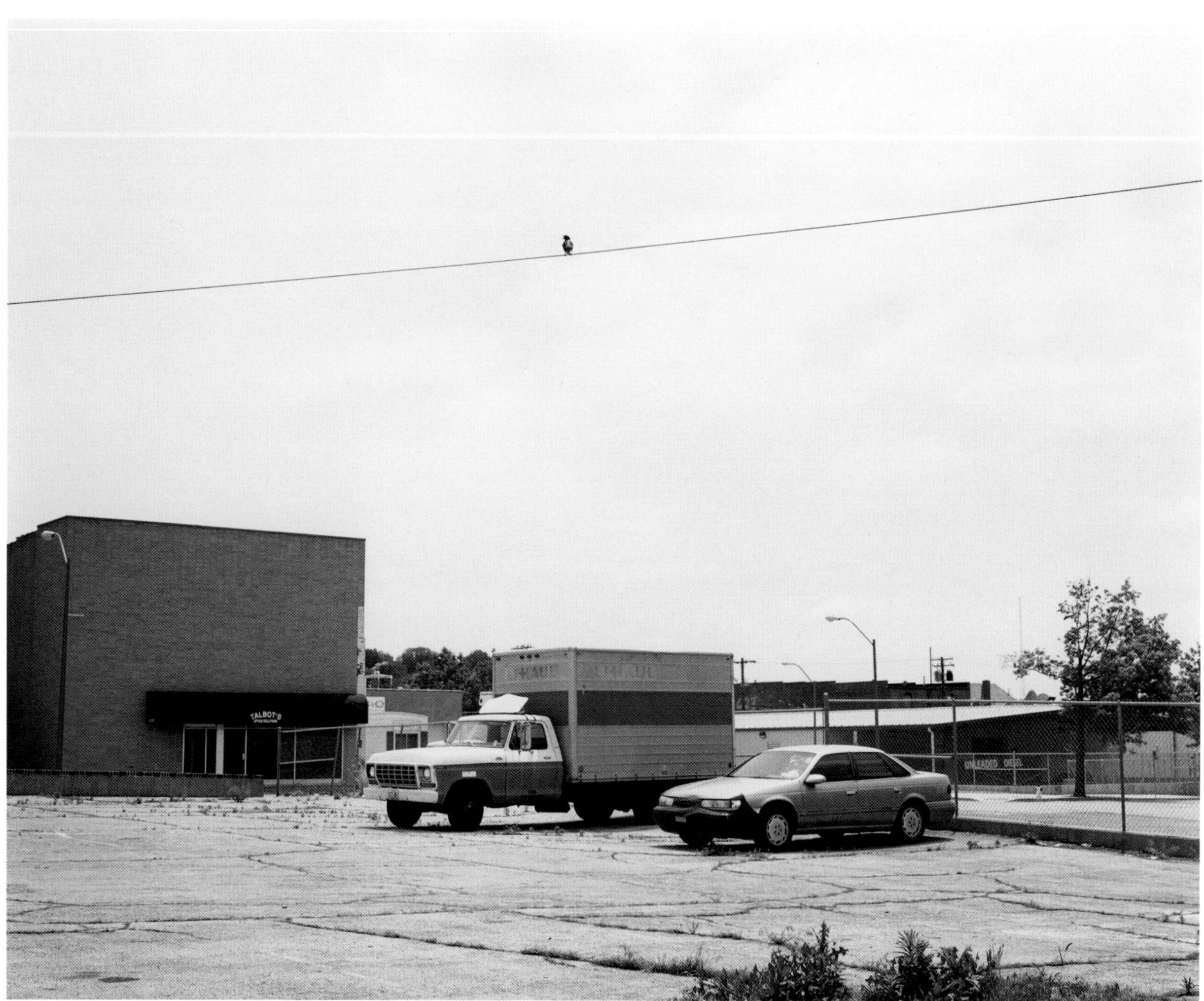

The most recent time I drove Highway 36 it was calving time in the meat-orchard, with the faintest powder of March snow on the hills. Near St. Francis, Kansas, I noticed that someone out there in all that space and sky had raised along the fenceline a new hand-made sign pointing to a historical site one mile north on Route 27—"the Cherry Creek Encampment"—that turned out to be a revelatory commemorative tablet honoring the devastated survivors of the Sand Creek Massacre who fled the scene that late November day and struck off to the northeast, eventually, after a hundred miles or so, to scratch a shallow camp in the diminutive creek valley thus marked, where they rested and healed themselves that lacerated winter of 1864. The memorial even carefully lists the individual Cheyennes by name, from Black Kettle and Blue Crane to Stuffed Gut and Spanish Woman. Such is the unexpected, omnidirectional generosity of the road and its tributaries and the pedigree of its handsome *côtes*.

Route 36 remains one of the more dignified means of crossing the mid-continent.

[FACING] *St. Joseph, Missouri*, Summer 2006

The stretch from Last Chance, Colorado, almost to St. Joseph, Missouri, is an unfettered, open-enough artery to finally attain the rhythm and syntax of, say, a river. But it is, of course, a line, a human beeline with daffodils and homefries, laughter and subtle wreck-age at its edges. Especially since frenetic Autobahn No. 70 to the near south trumped much of the aggressive hucksterism from 36's curbs, the latter has acquired an insouciant, "There but for the grace of God," shunpike bearing, which, combined with its vistas and its almost instant archaeological status, makes it a trajectory capable of both inspiring and reciprocating a simple, honest affection.

Those high plains, the *côtes* above the would-be river, remain a classical locus for vast exhalation and contemplative sway: the impeccable straightaways and the hawks over-head. The prairie cottonwoods, many times the wildest creatures in sight, carry the ensign of vertical life: twisted and tongue-tied, both blind and curious, always with the appear-ance of trying to pull up roots and hobble away. Even the dullest reaches of merciless cor-porate agriculture can be put to good use sizing the cloud realm, or practicing bird sounds at the wheel, in the grand tradition of Li Po's "One of us calls out in partridge song."

I relinquished some time ago most efforts to persuade skeptics of the high-sailing beauty of such as-the-crow-flies spaces and the restorative passage through them, writing the whole thing off as a capacity similar to distinguishing carmine from crimson, off-bronze from old palomino. But it seems continually necessary to reassert that landscape study and its reflective arts are anything but passive disciplines, that civilization in a sustaining, daily sense emerges most surely from good relations with one's surroundings (the perfect word) and the inner landscape of possibility held in the head and heart.

Bill Wylie's recent 36 crossings-with-camera remint all of this: the region's great capacity for inflection, double take, and surprise. The humble aplomb of things-in-waiting: a preposterous barn, lights on the skyline half crazy with neglect. And the benignity of a deftly cast eye.

These photos incite me to drive back out there, come May or October, if I can wait that long, to reaffirm just how those raggedy cedars hug the edges of those infinitely particular ridge lines, and to watch as the Arikaree, the Beaver, the Sappa, and then the Prairie Dog creeks make their forbearing, undeniable ways from the uplands, how they hedge and parry, feint and hook . . . To reaffirm an intelligent planet whereon one might even, with luck, breathe an intelligent breath, drive an intelligent mile, set an intelligent foot.

1 *Prairie west of Blakeman, Kansas*, Summer 2006

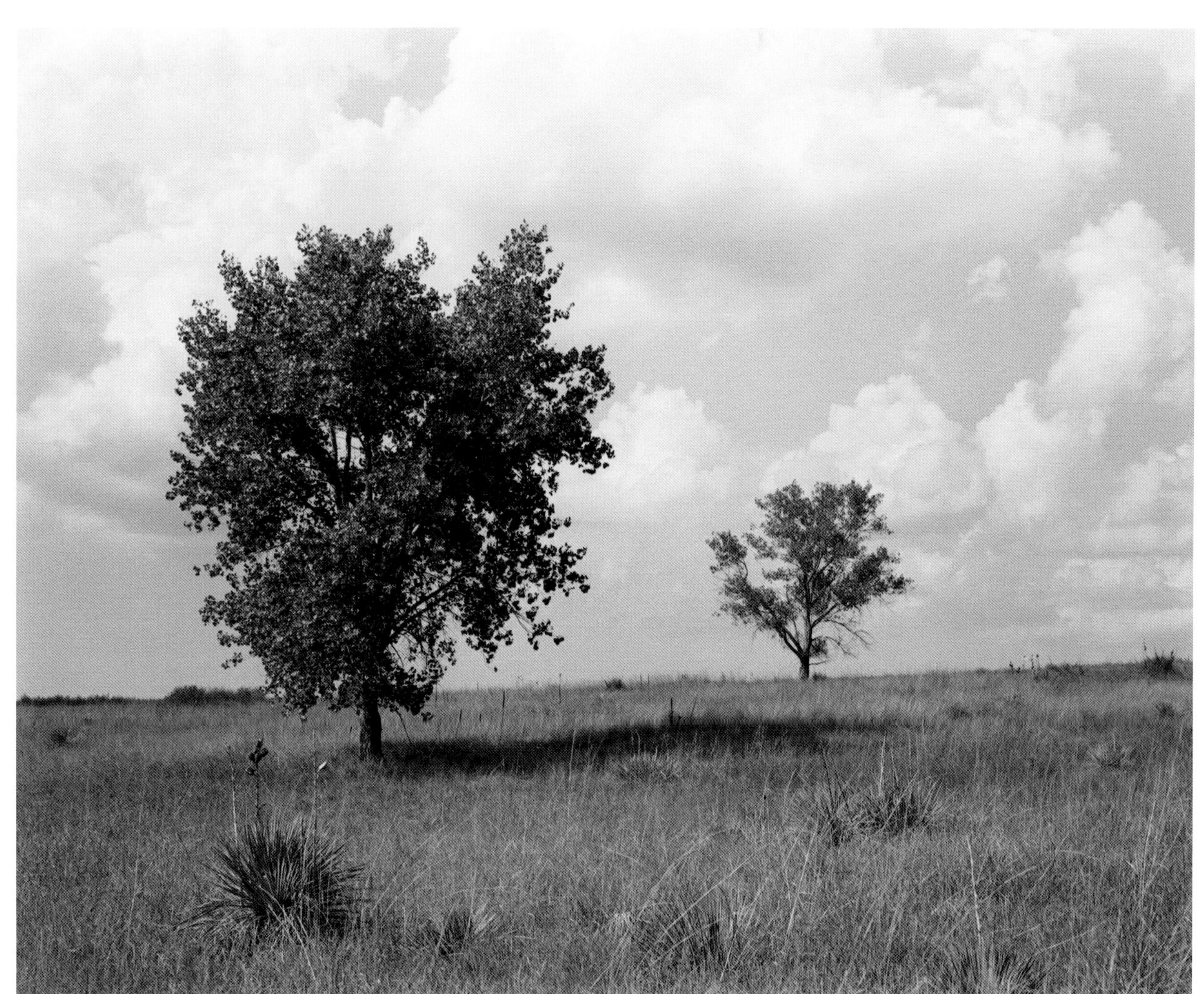

2 *Near Courtland, Kansas*, Summer 2007

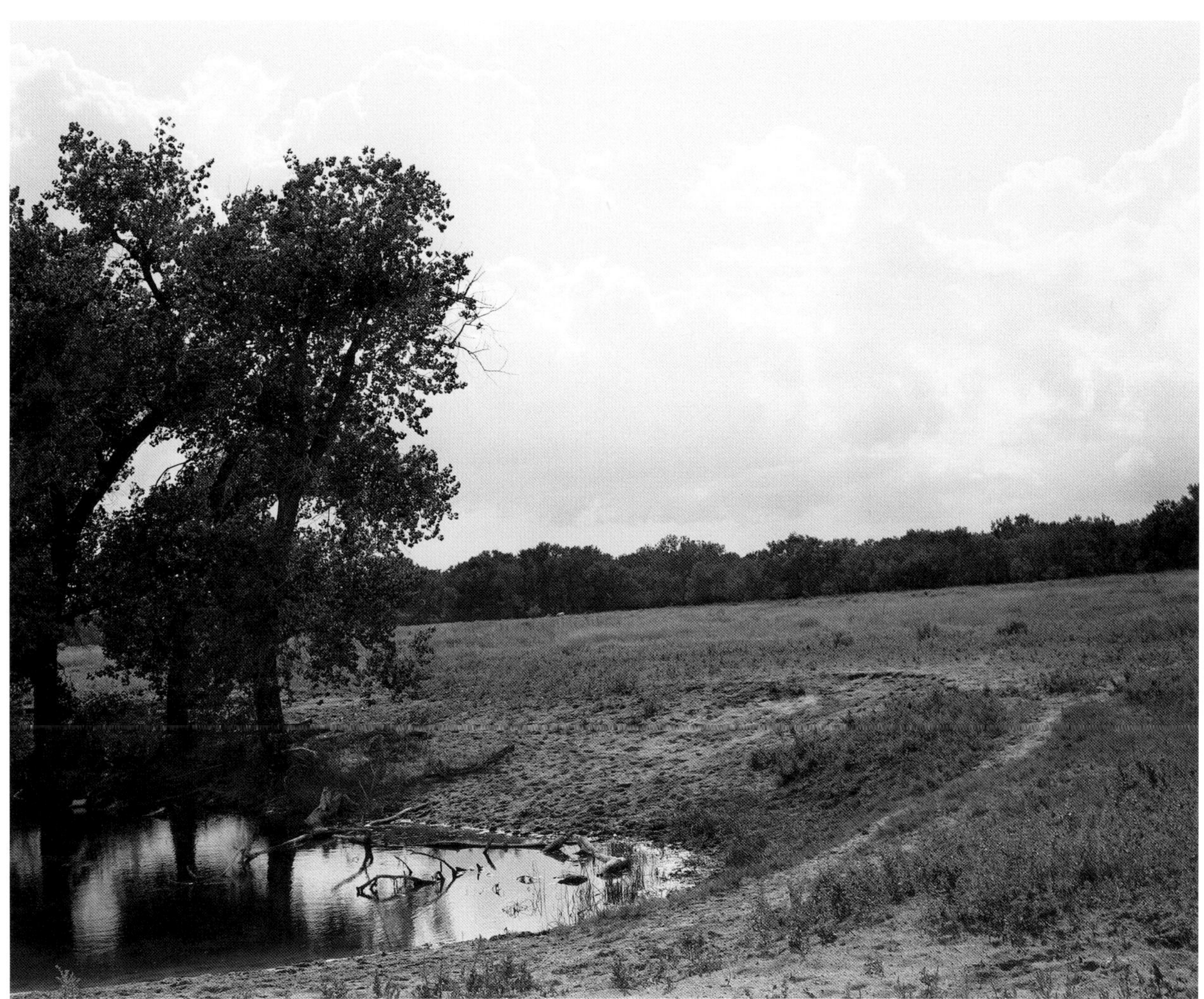

3 *Near Wathena, Kansas,* Summer 2006

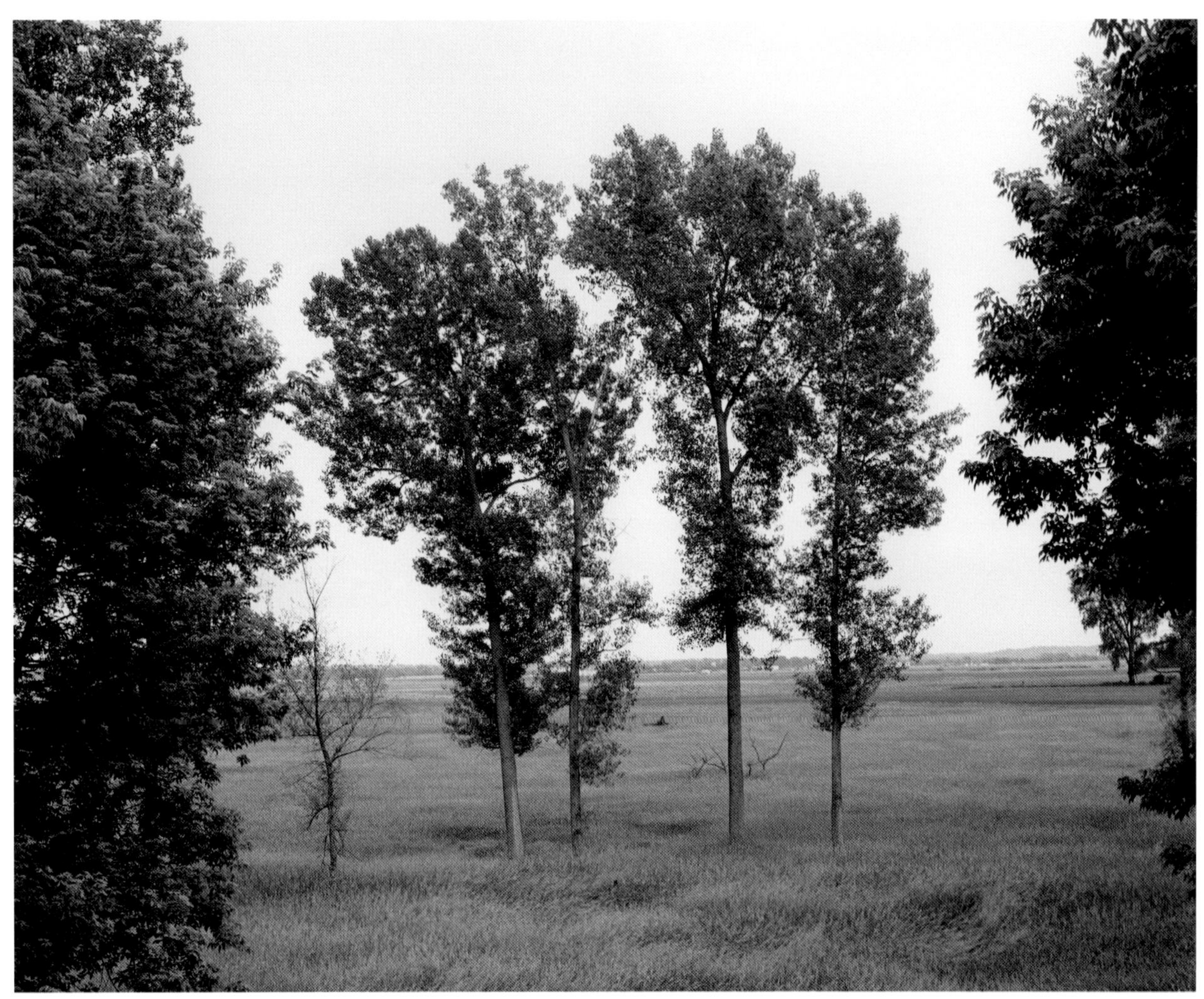

4 *McDonald, Kansas*, Summer 2007

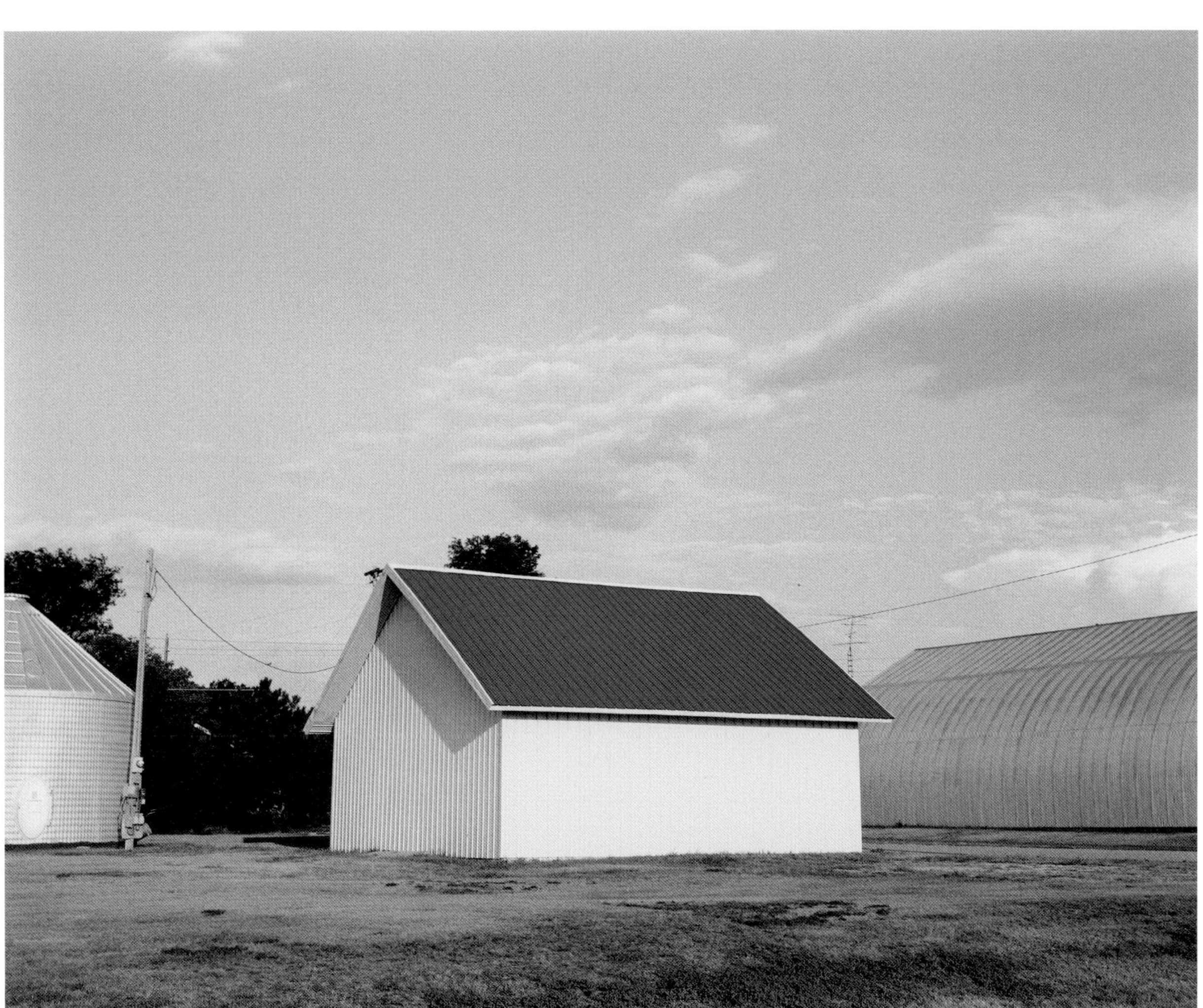

5 *Bird City, Kansas*, Fall 2005

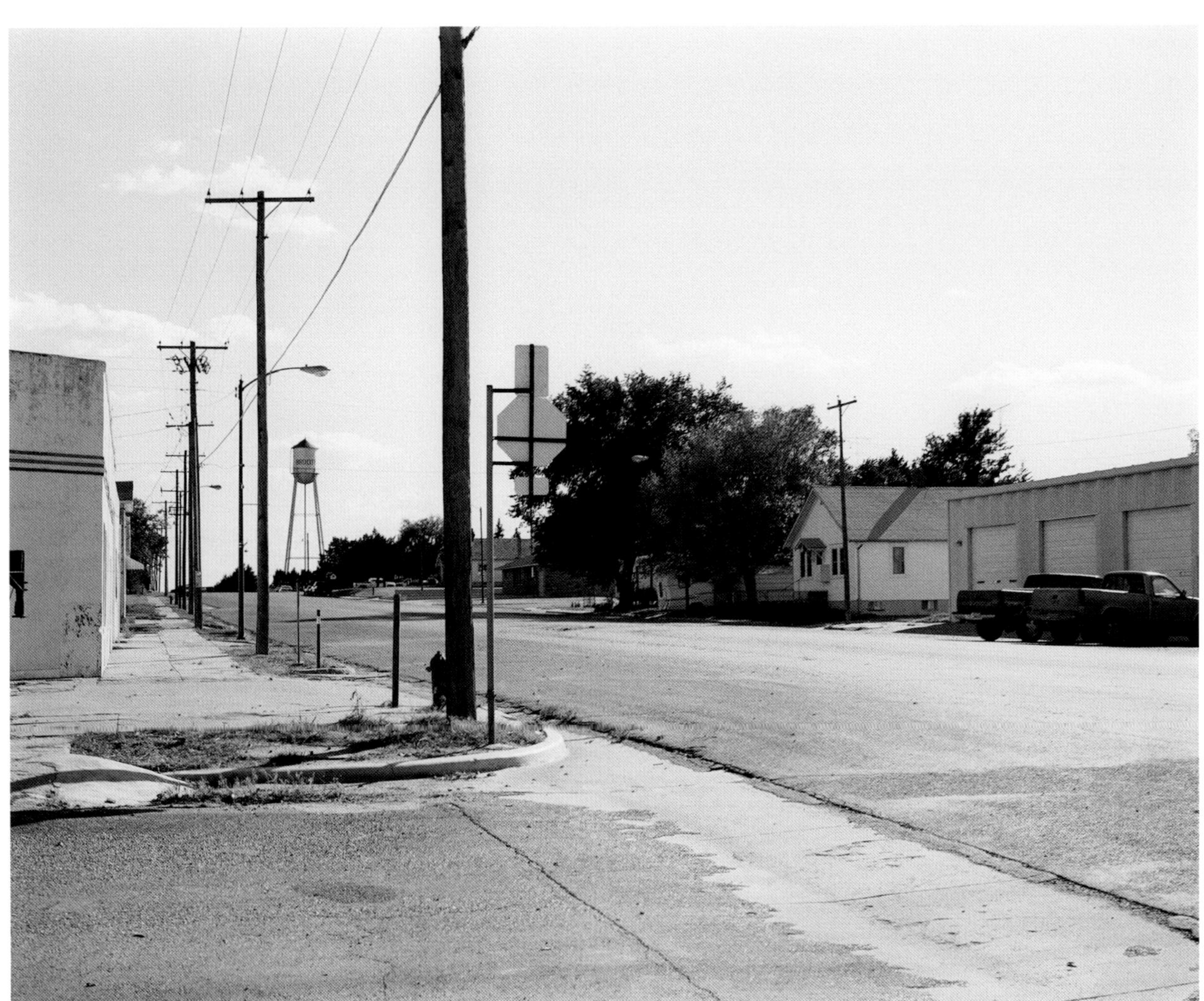

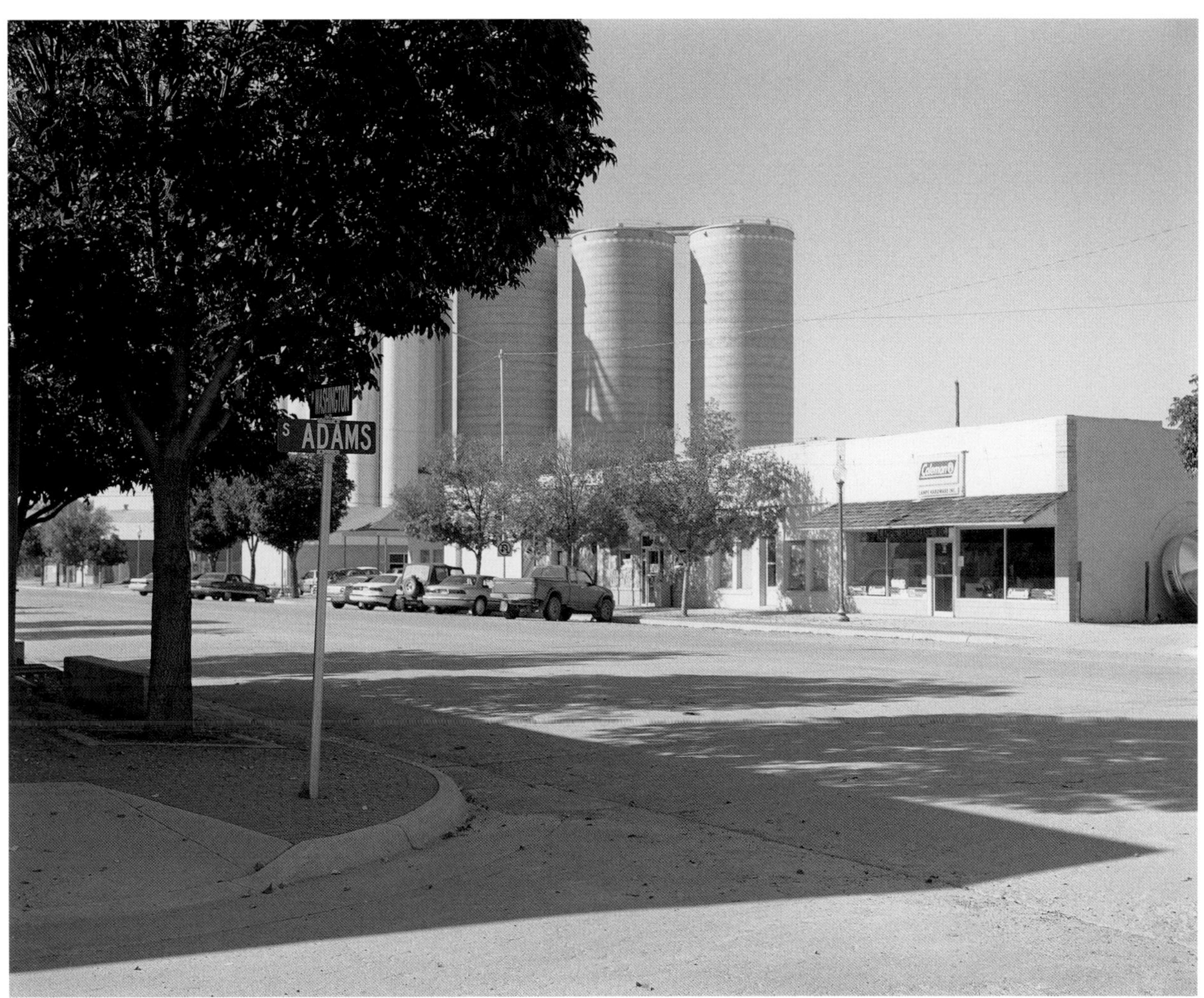

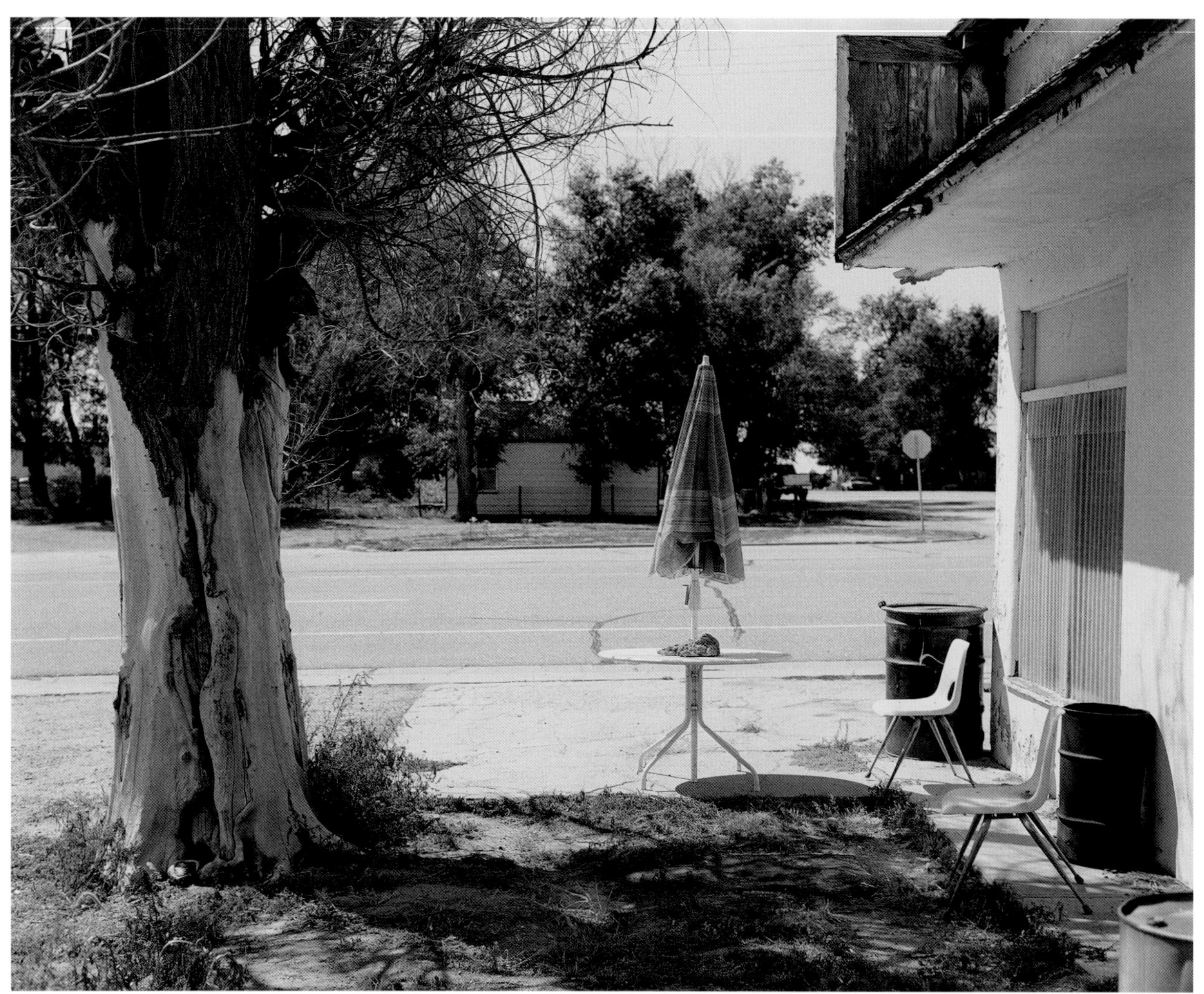

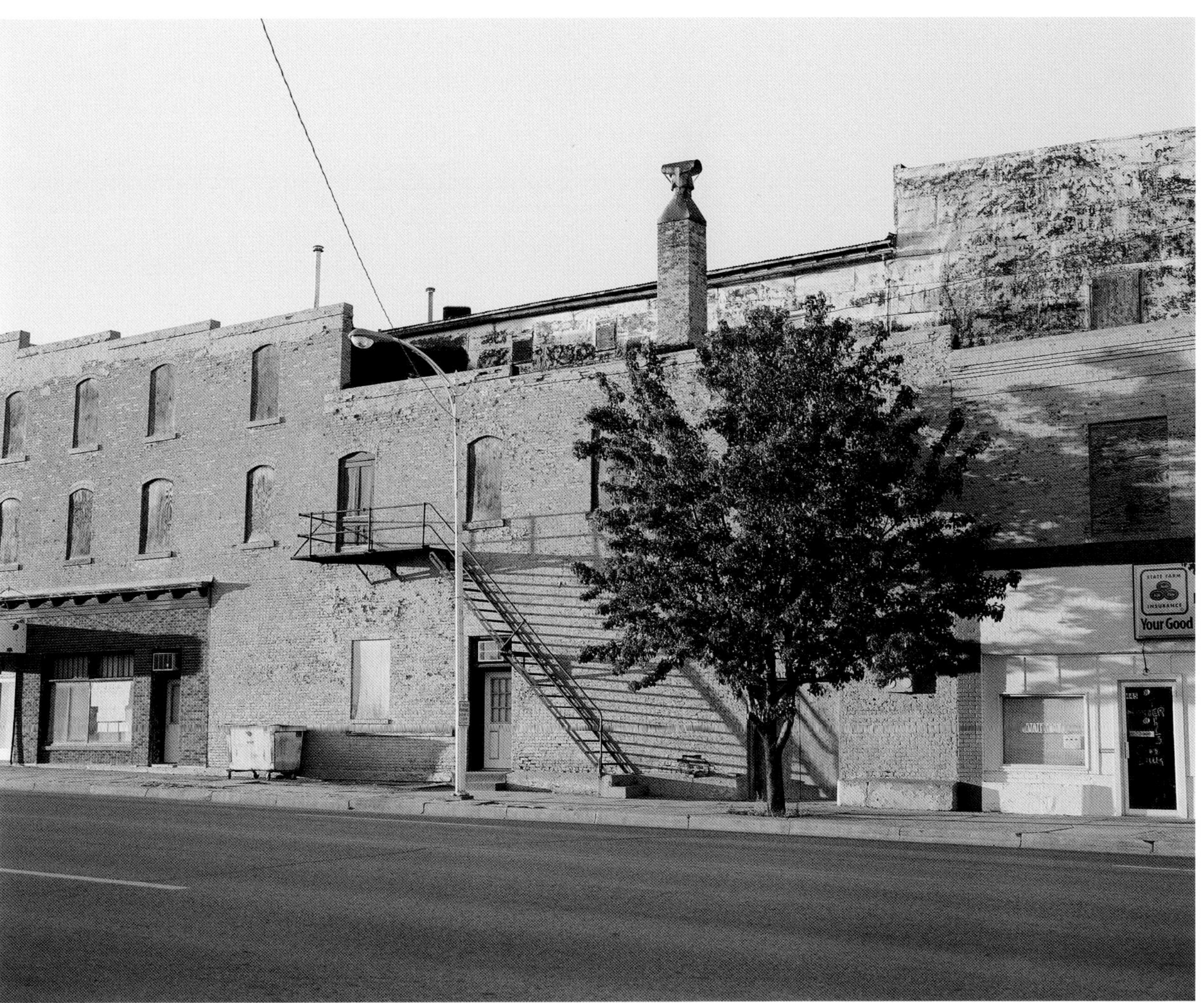
STATE FARM
INSURANCE
Your Good

9 *Near Home, Kansas*, Summer 2007

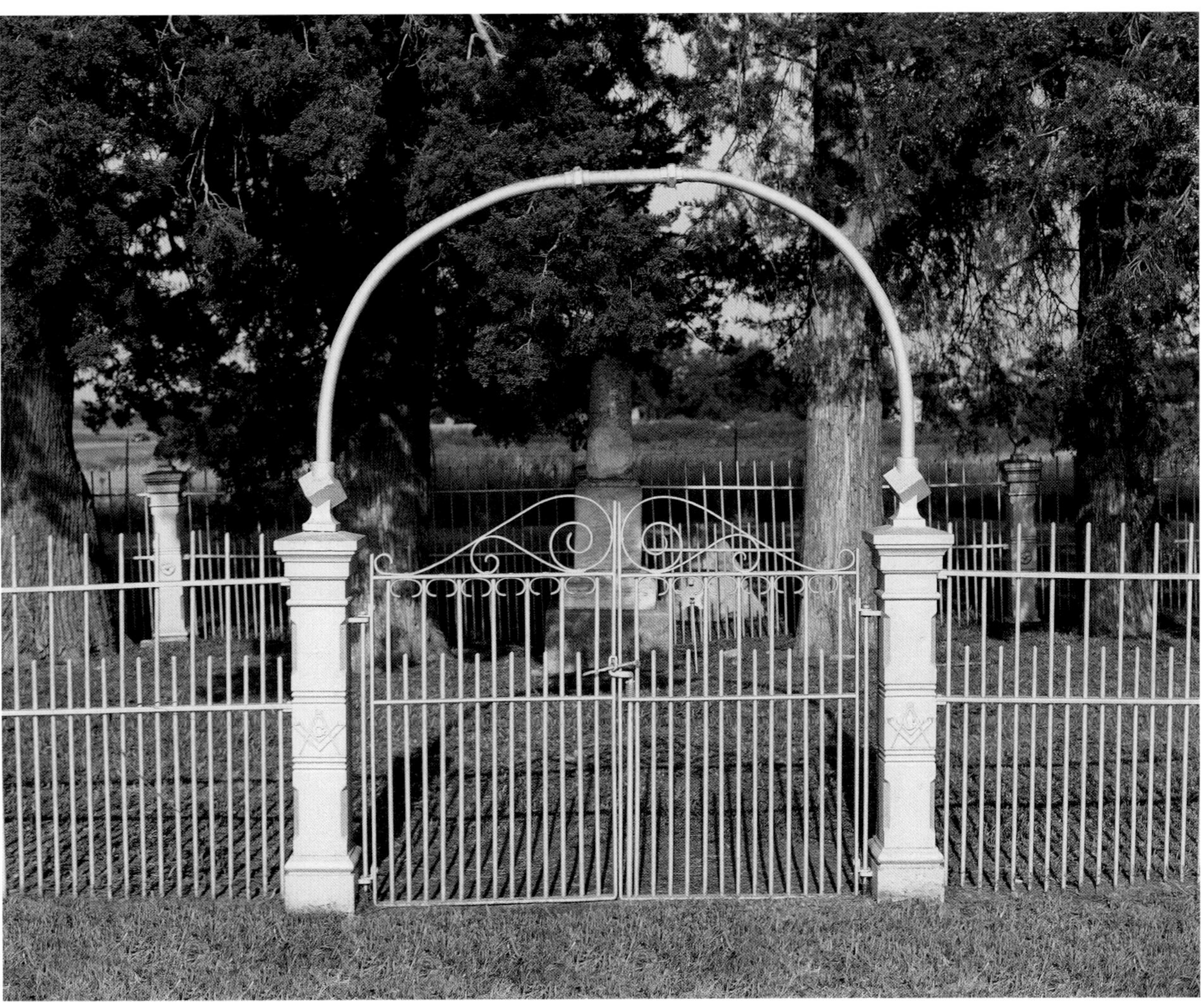

10 *Near Axtell, Kansas,* Summer 2007

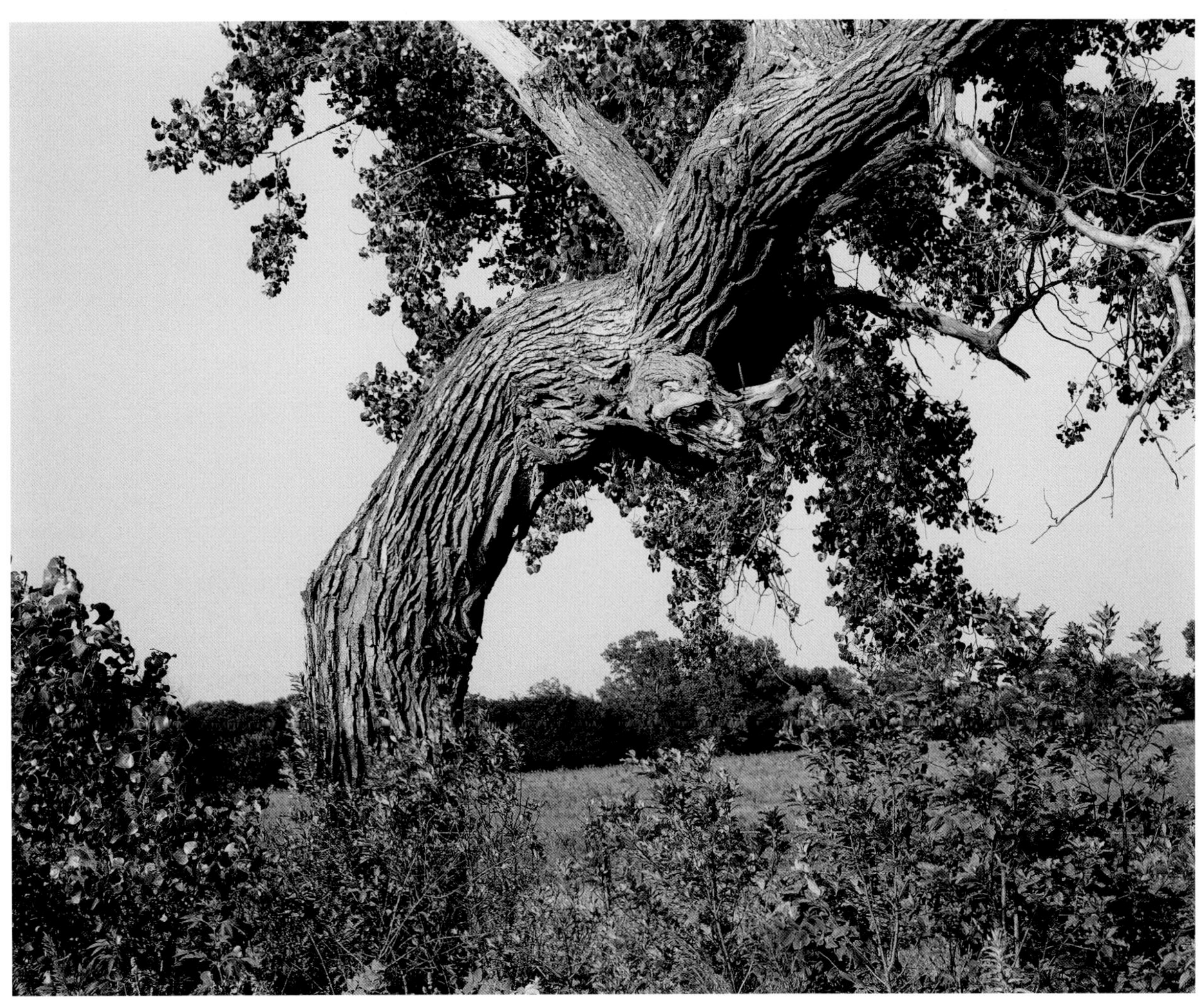

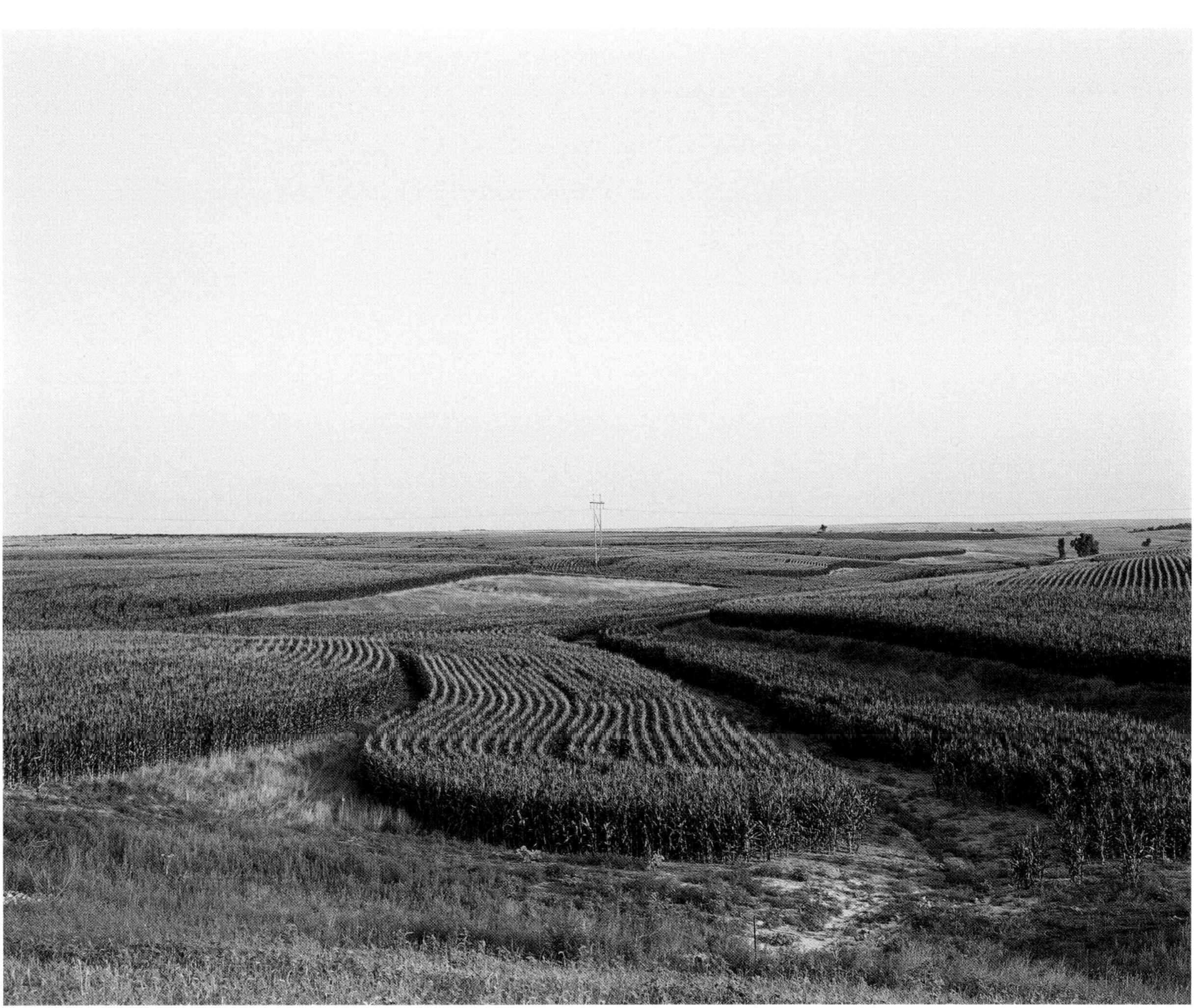

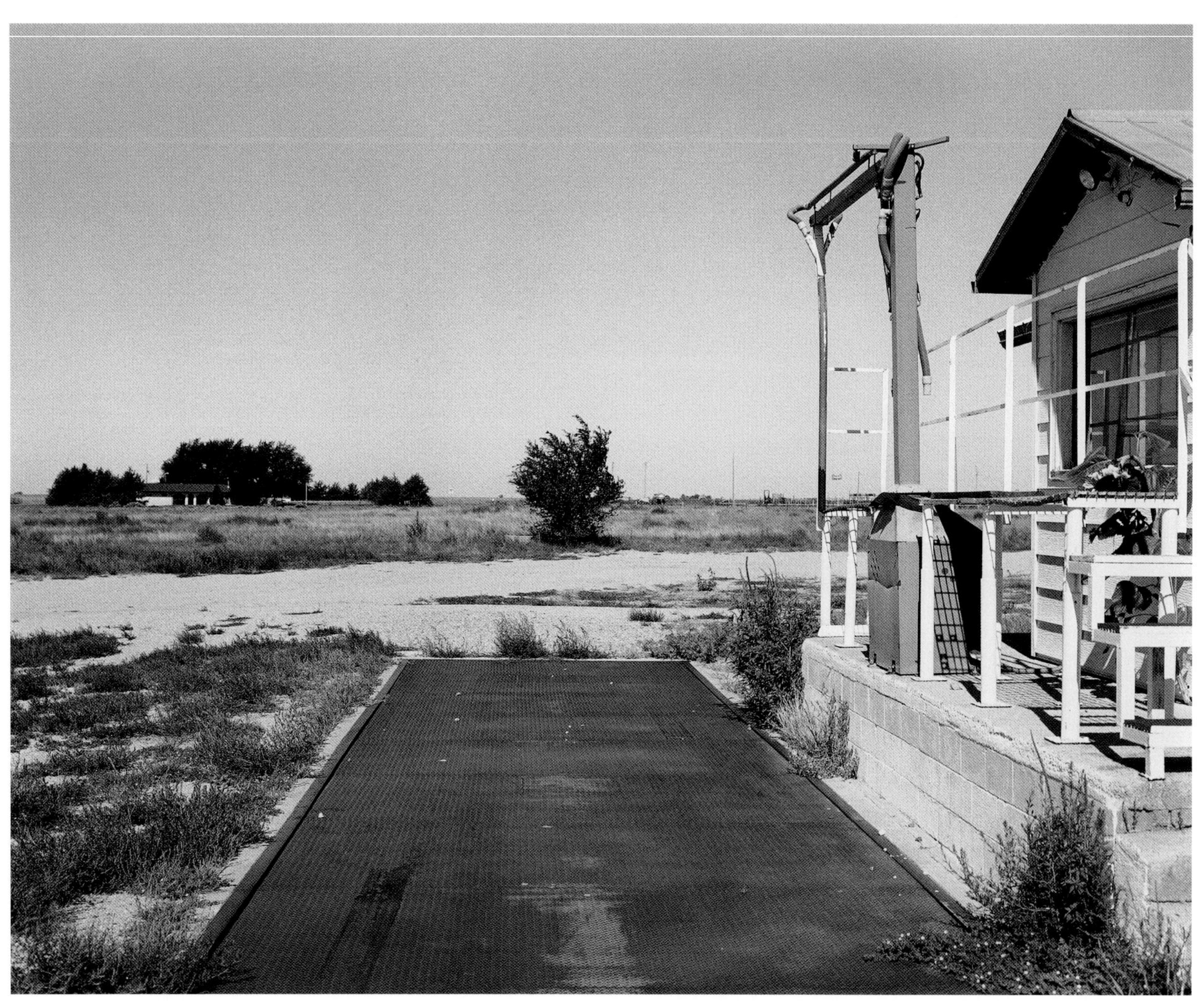

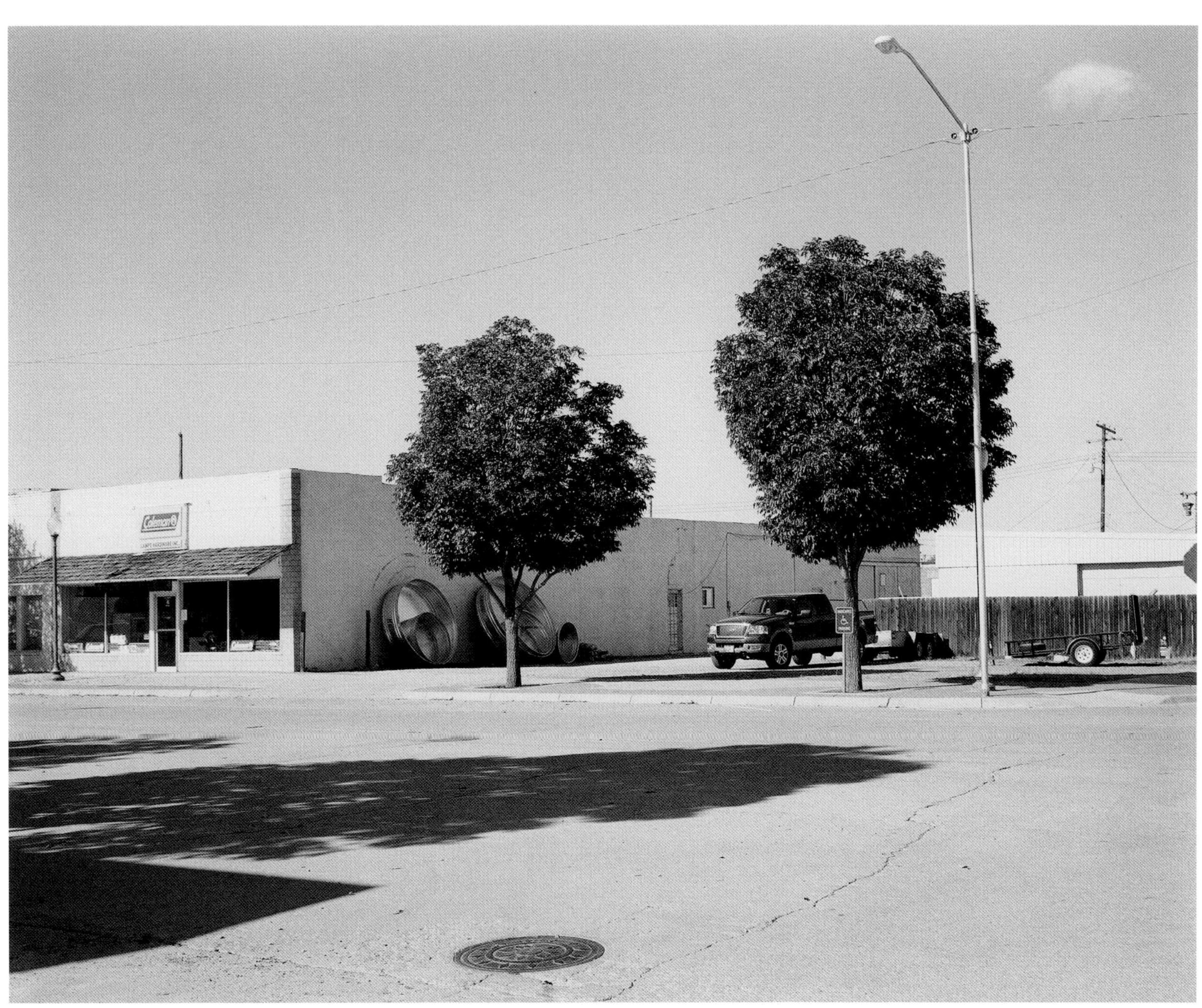

14 *Beattie, Kansas,* Summer 2008

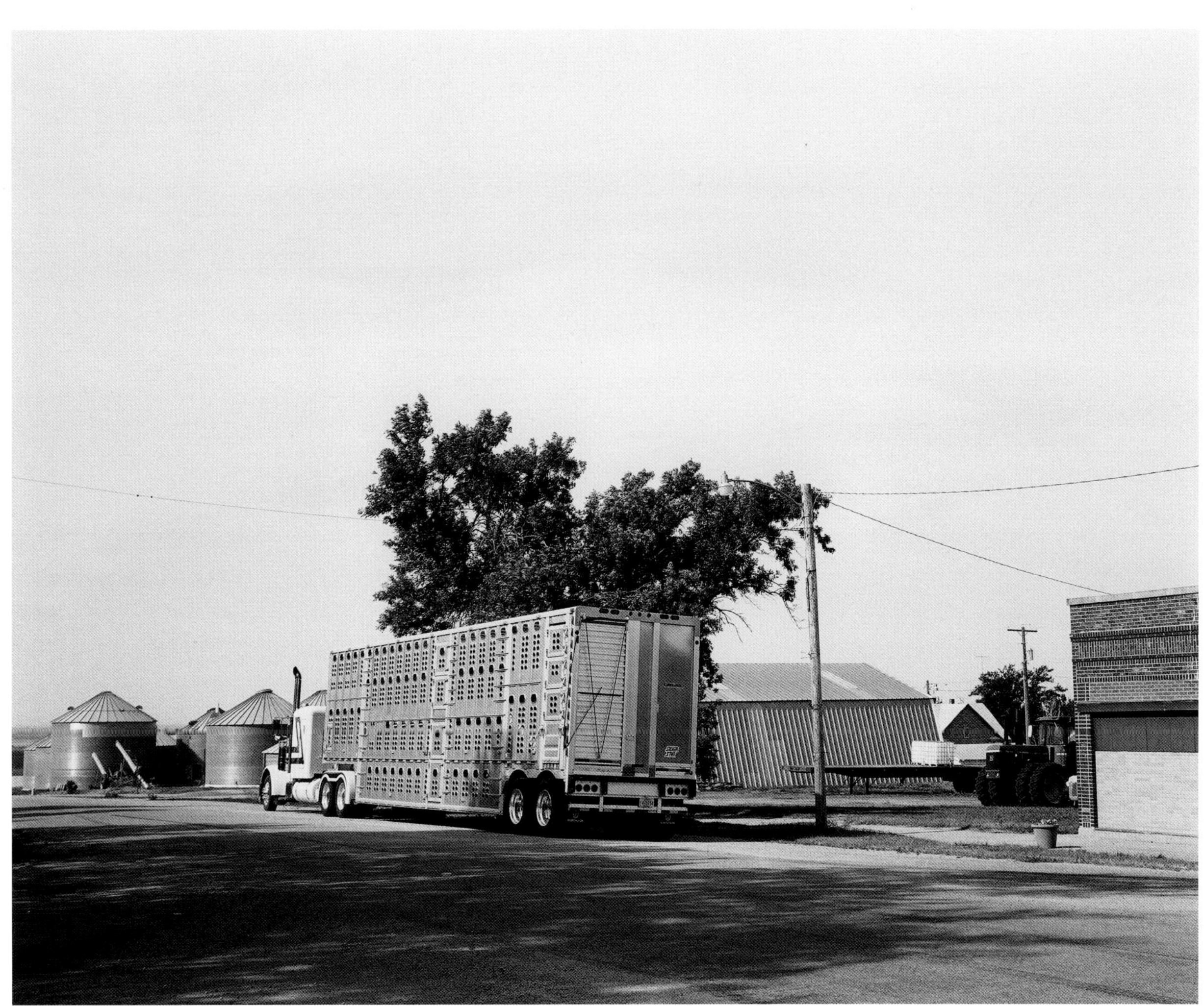

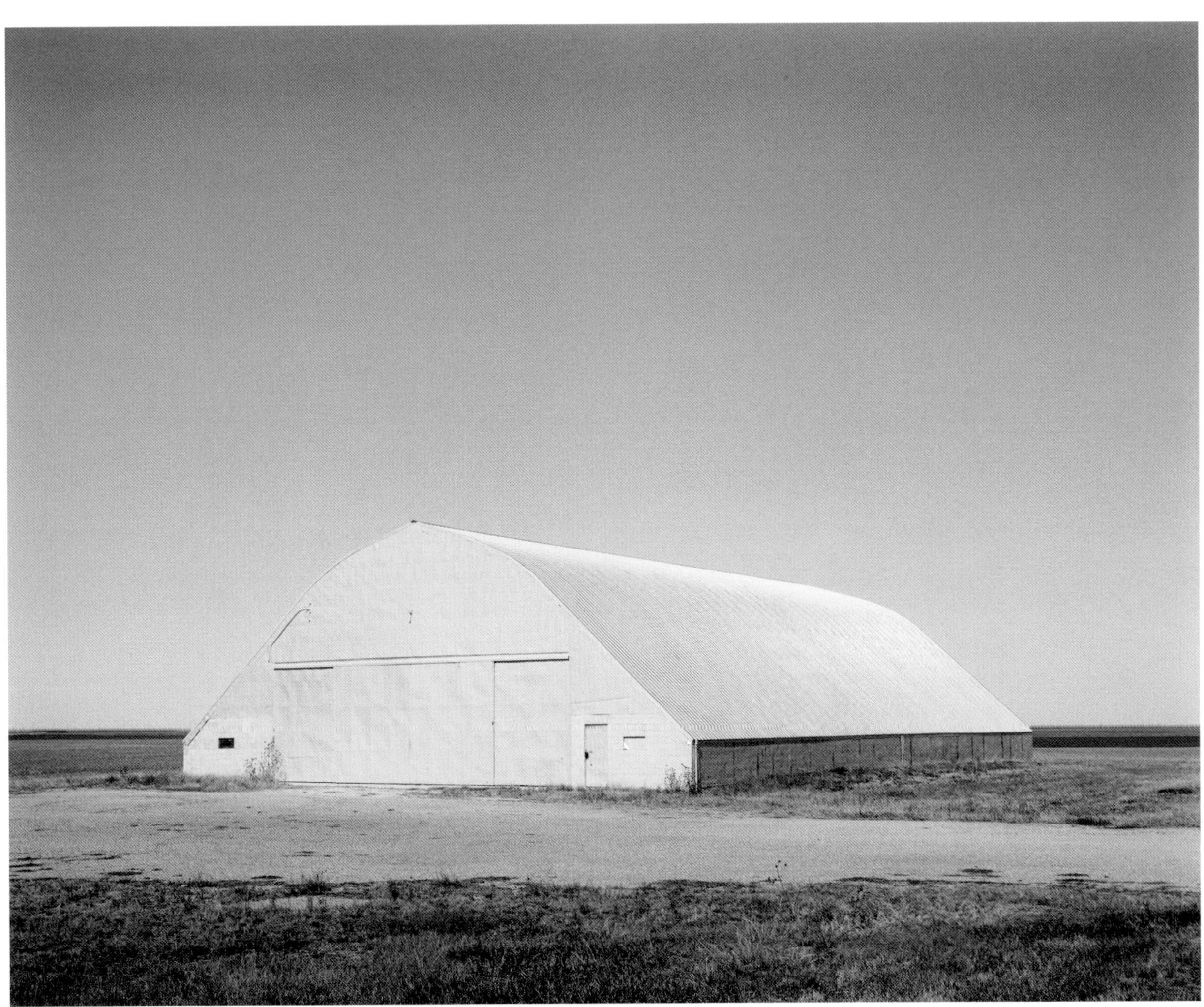

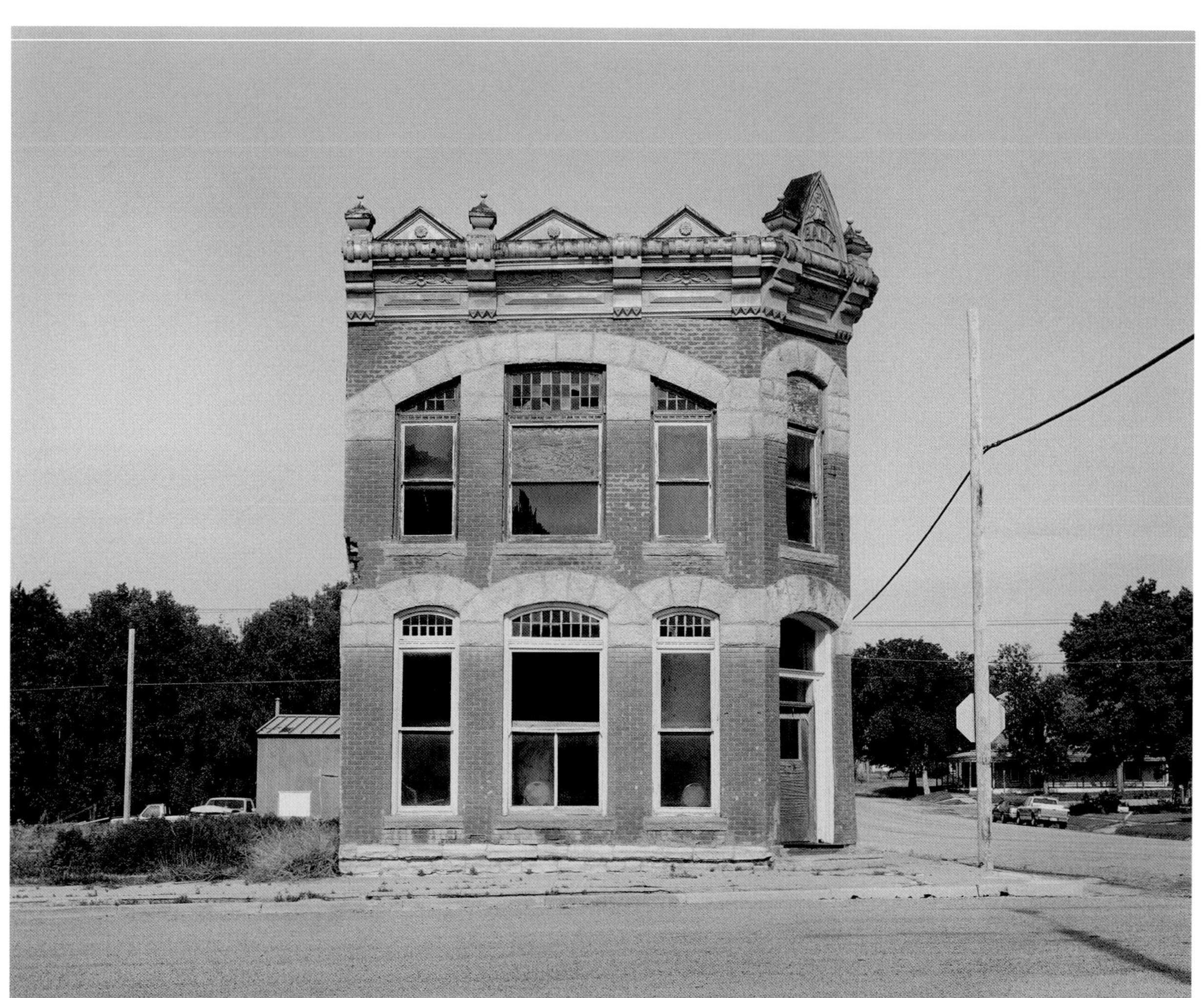

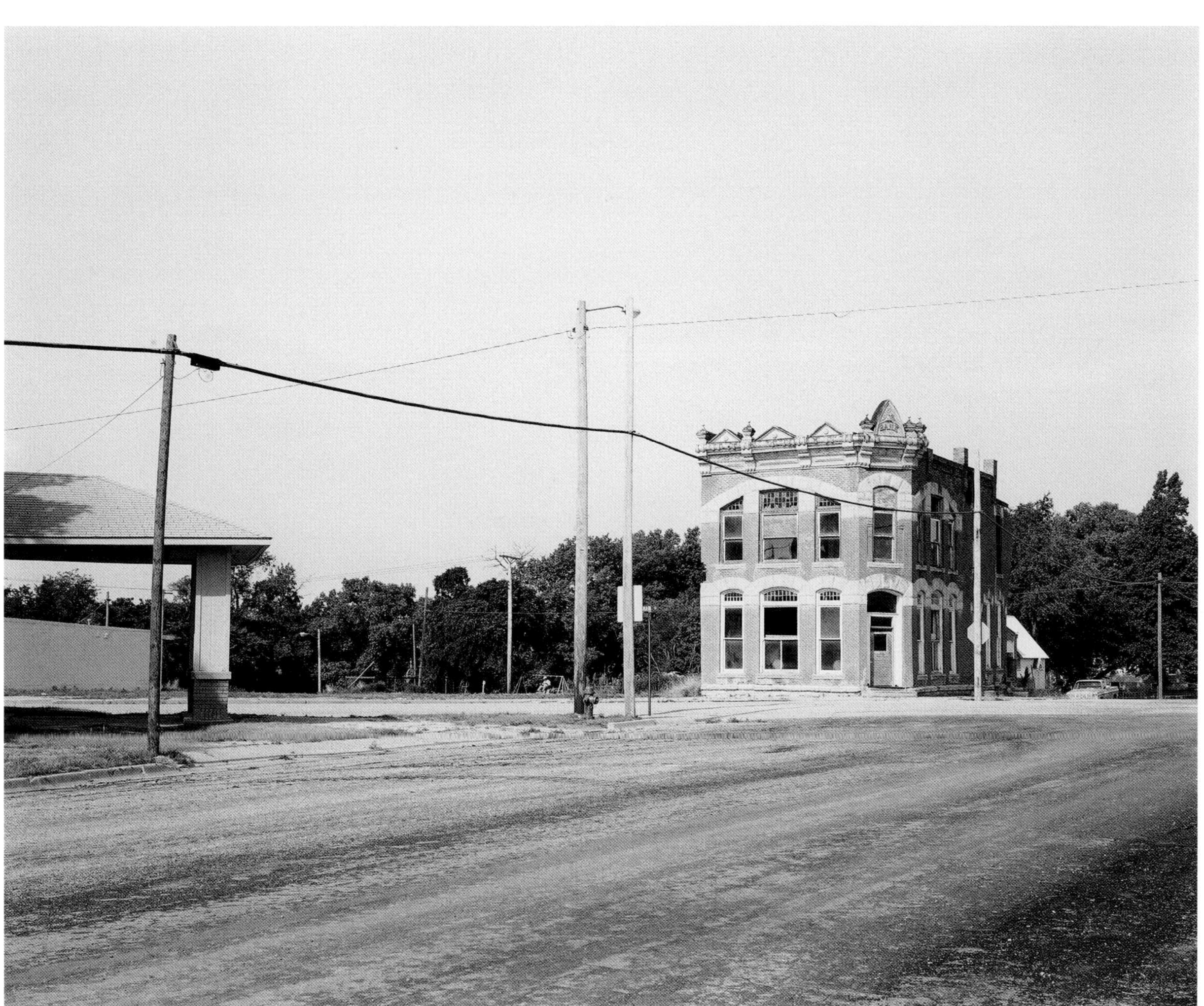

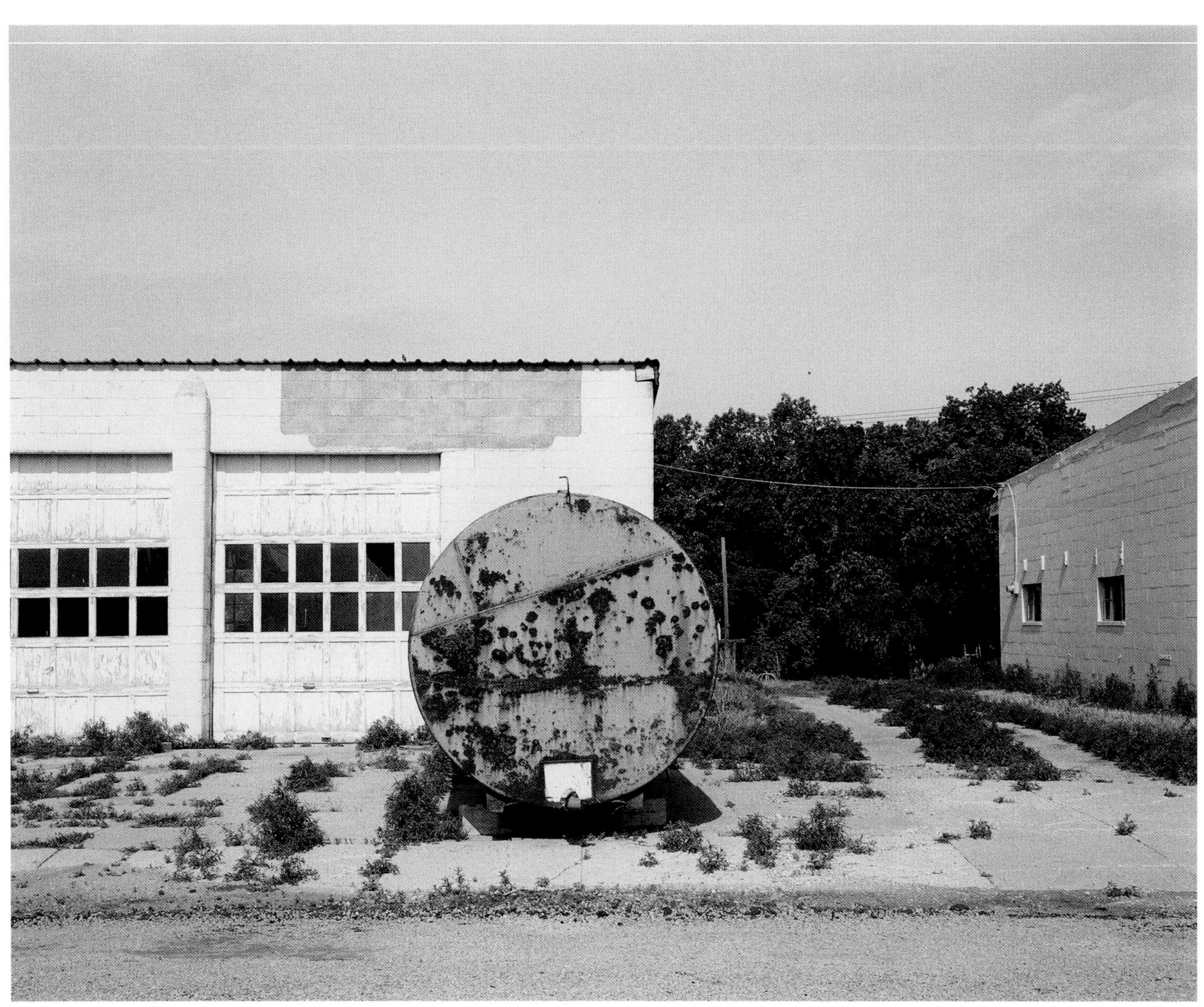

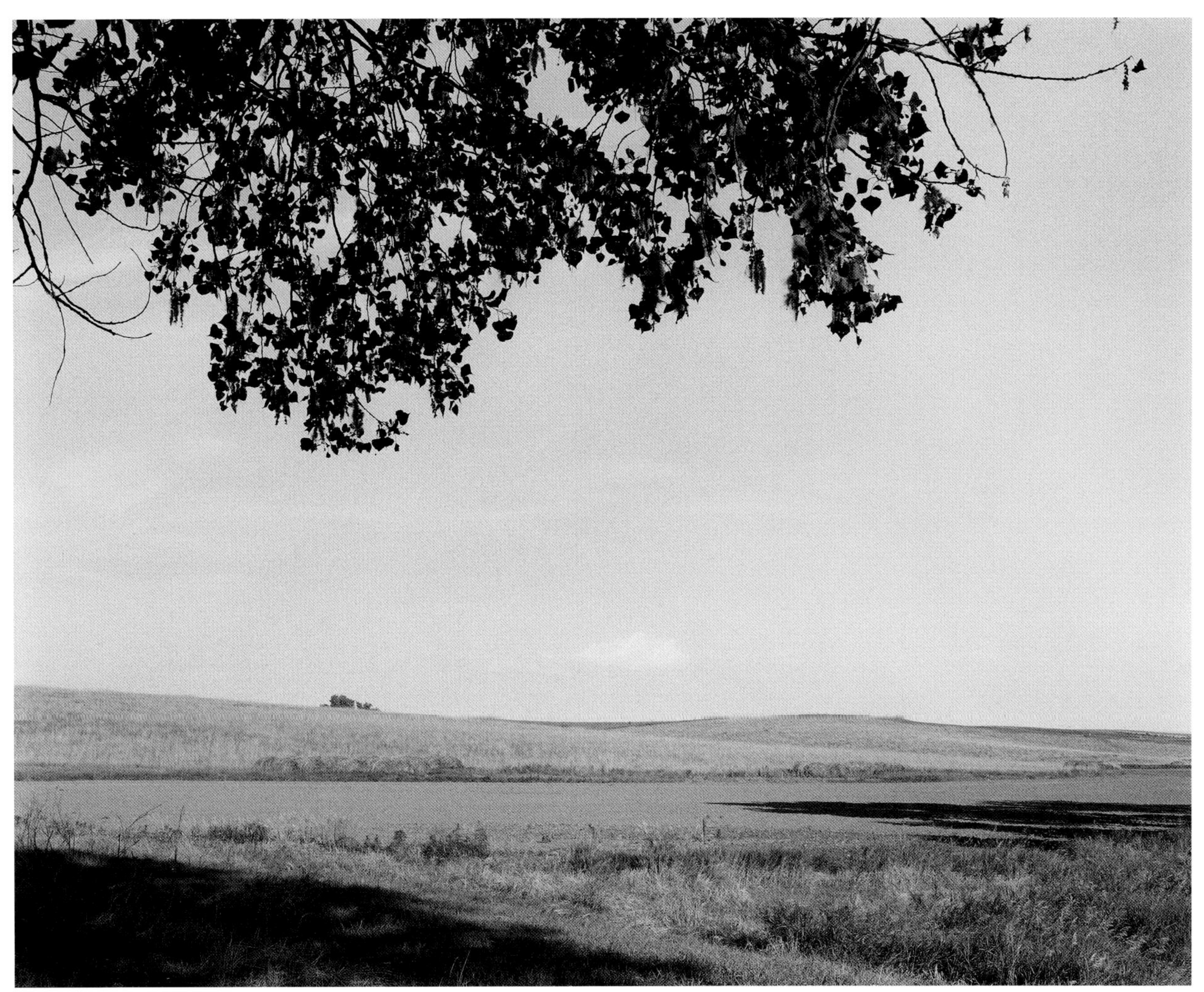

20 *Near Ludell, Kansas,* Summer 2008

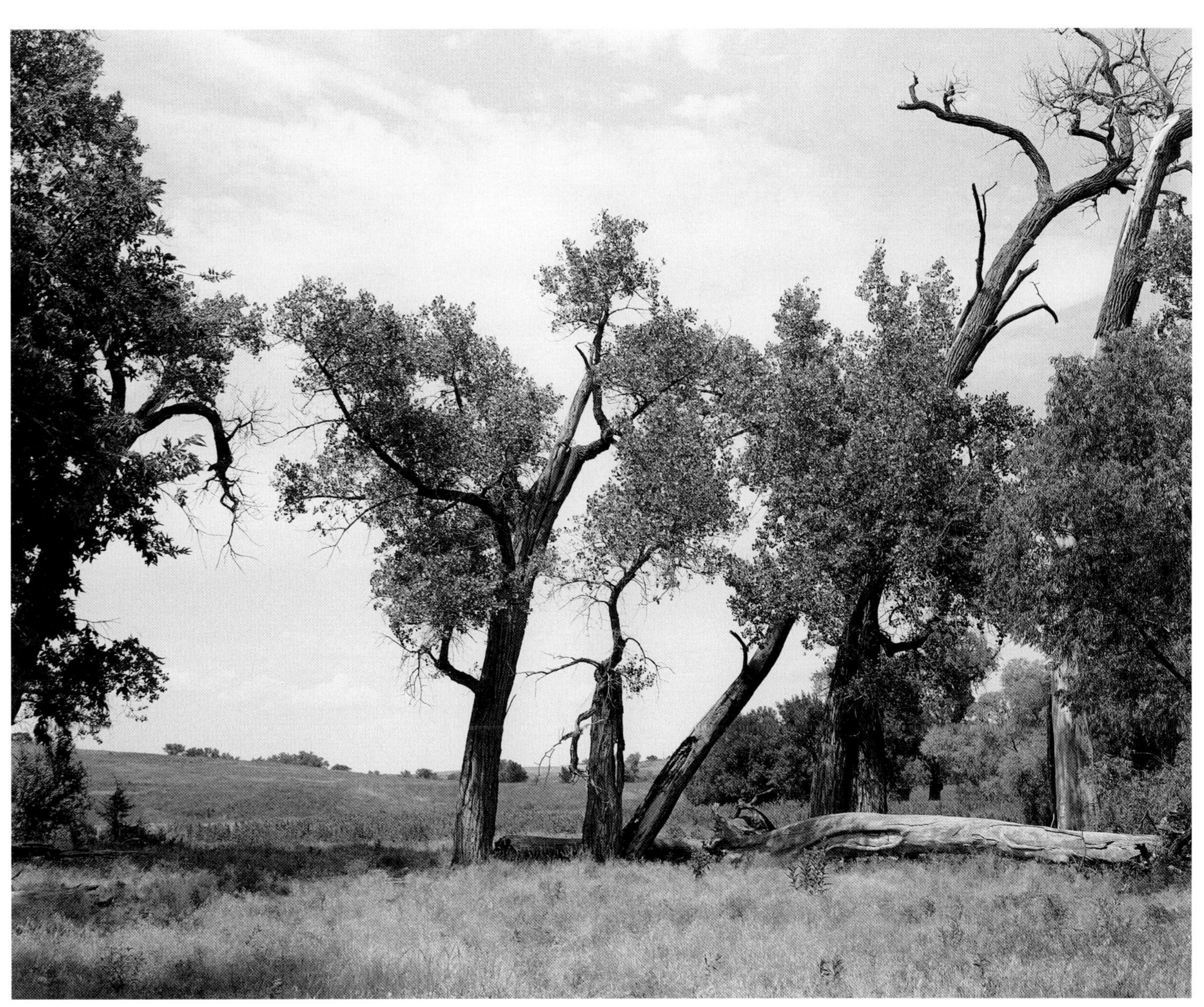

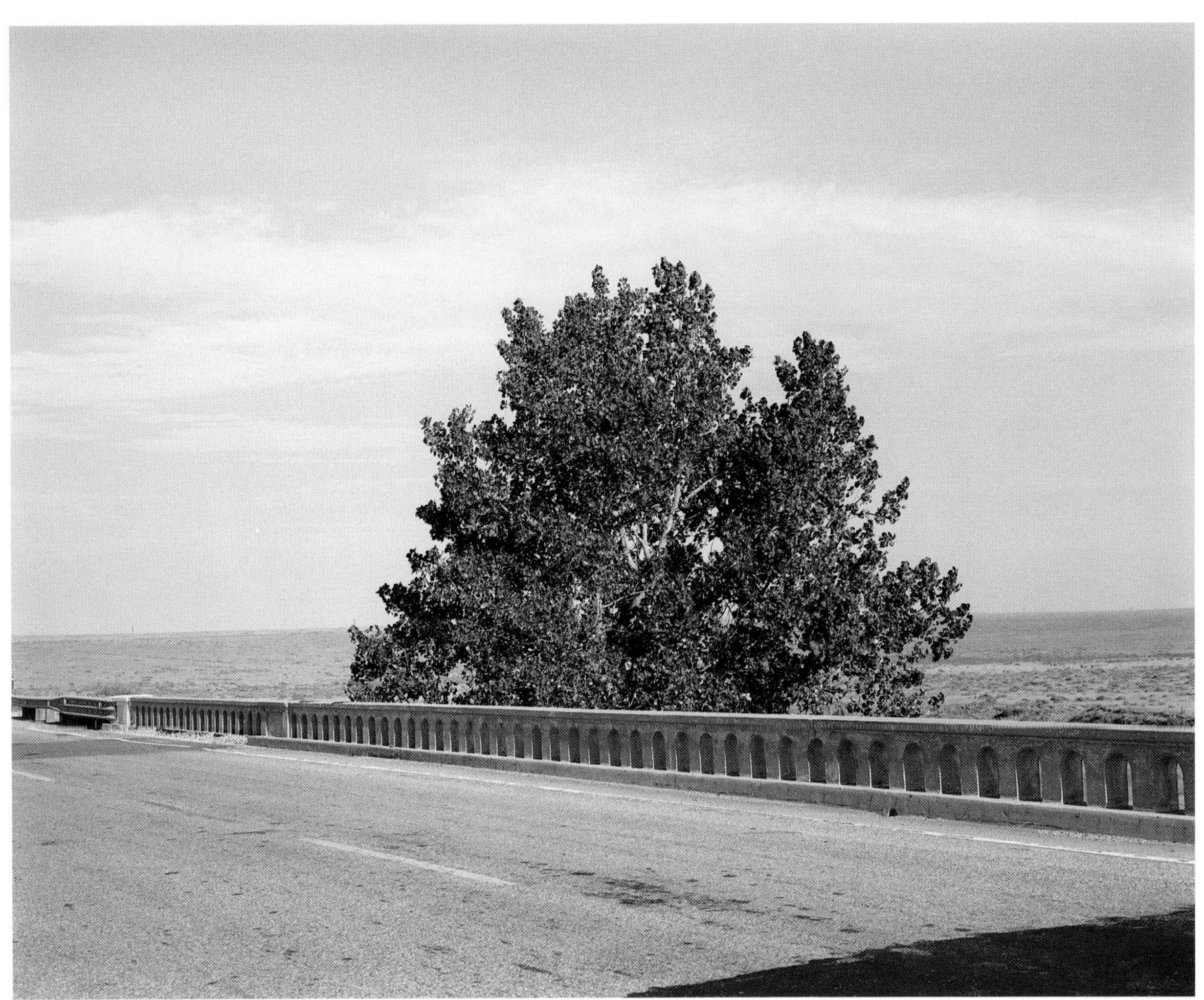

22 *Near Atwood, Kansas,* Summer 2007

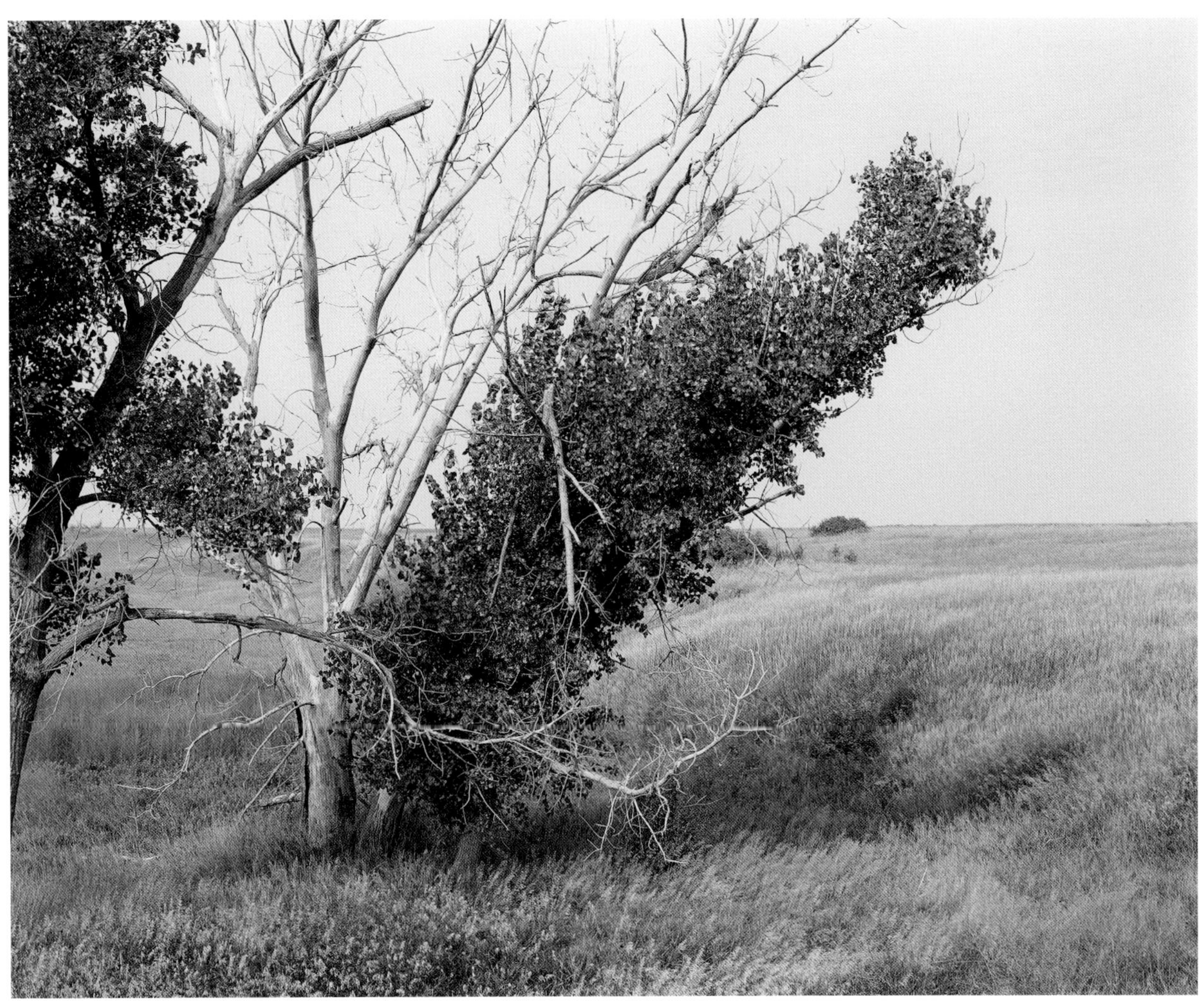

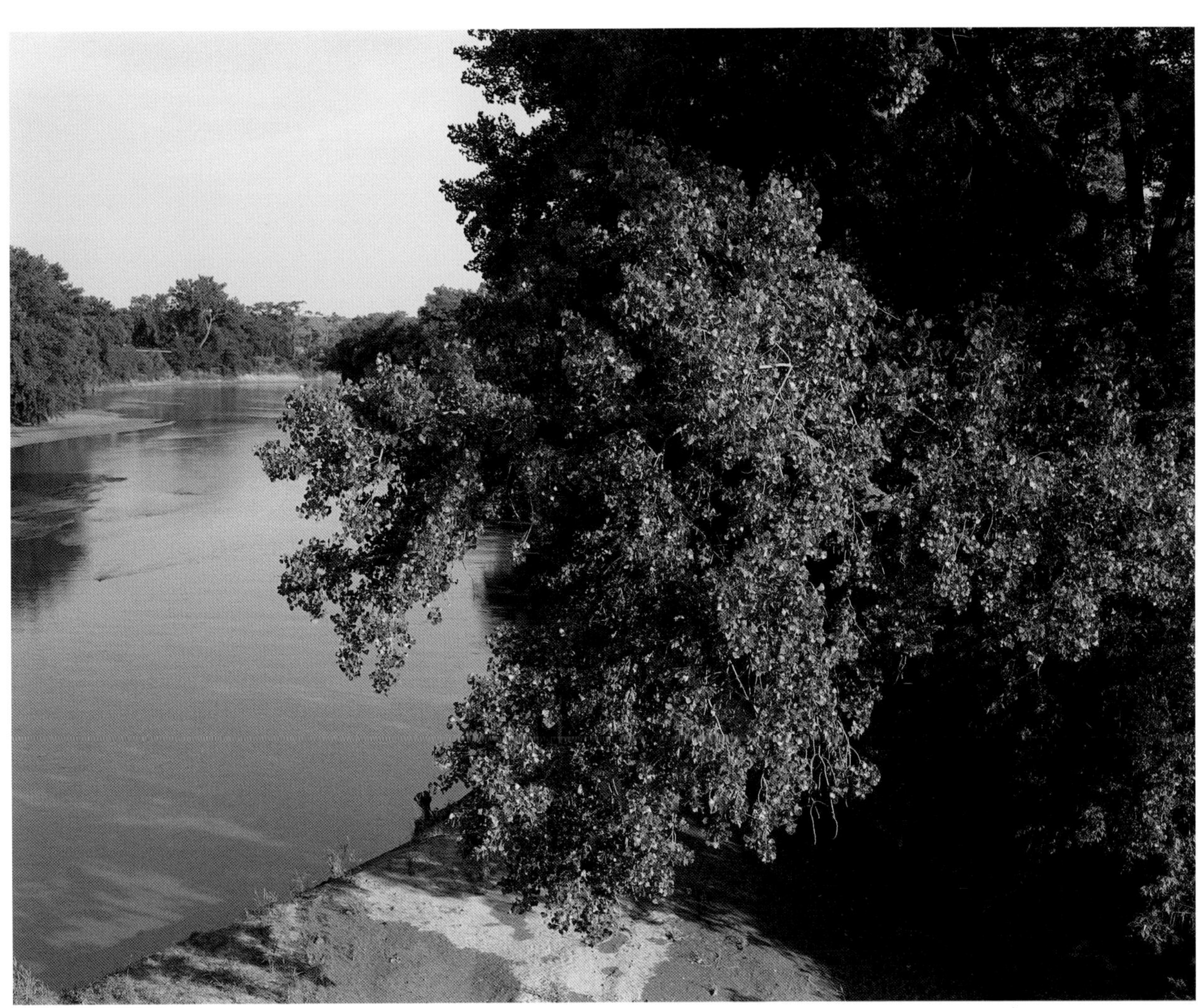

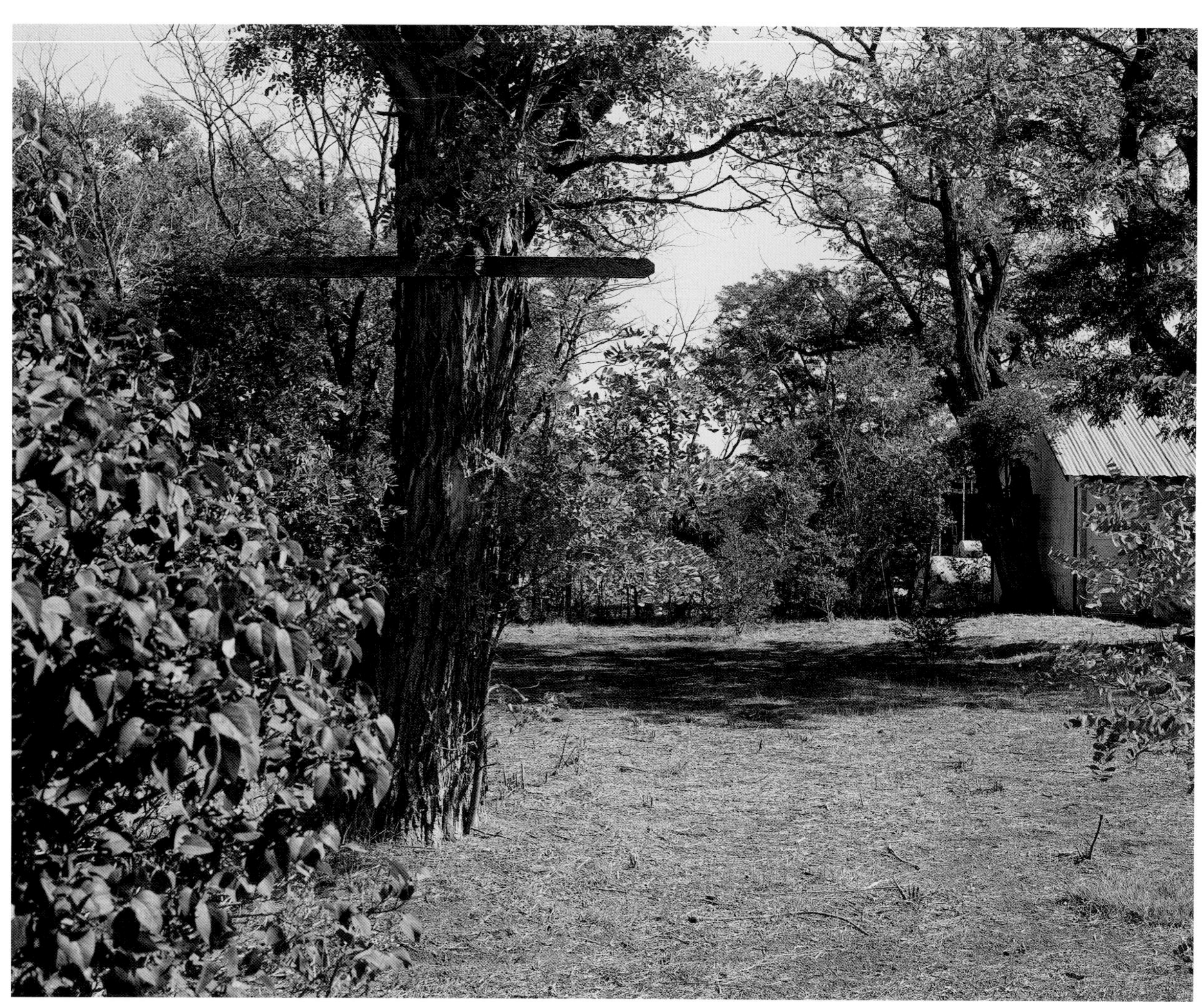

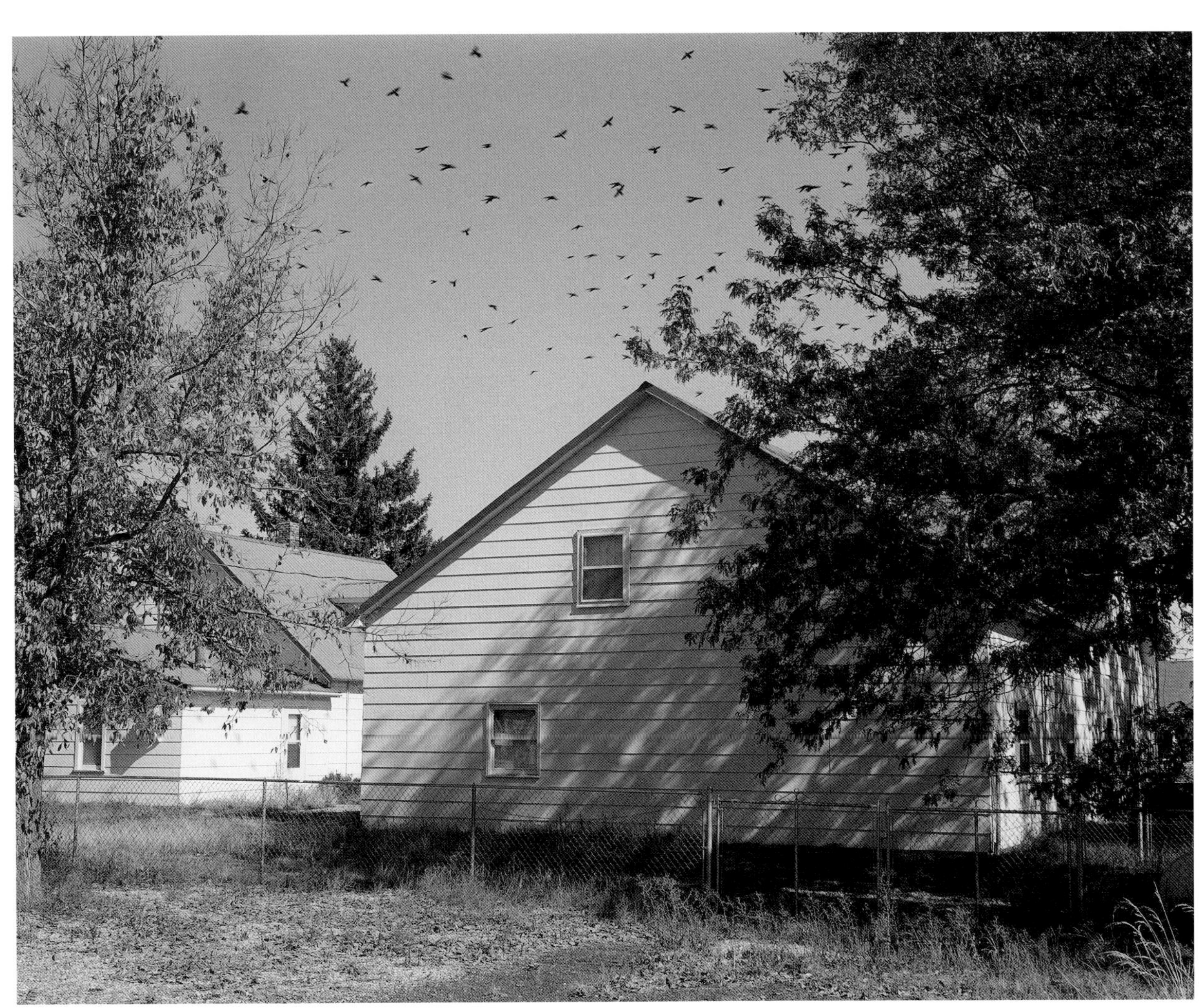

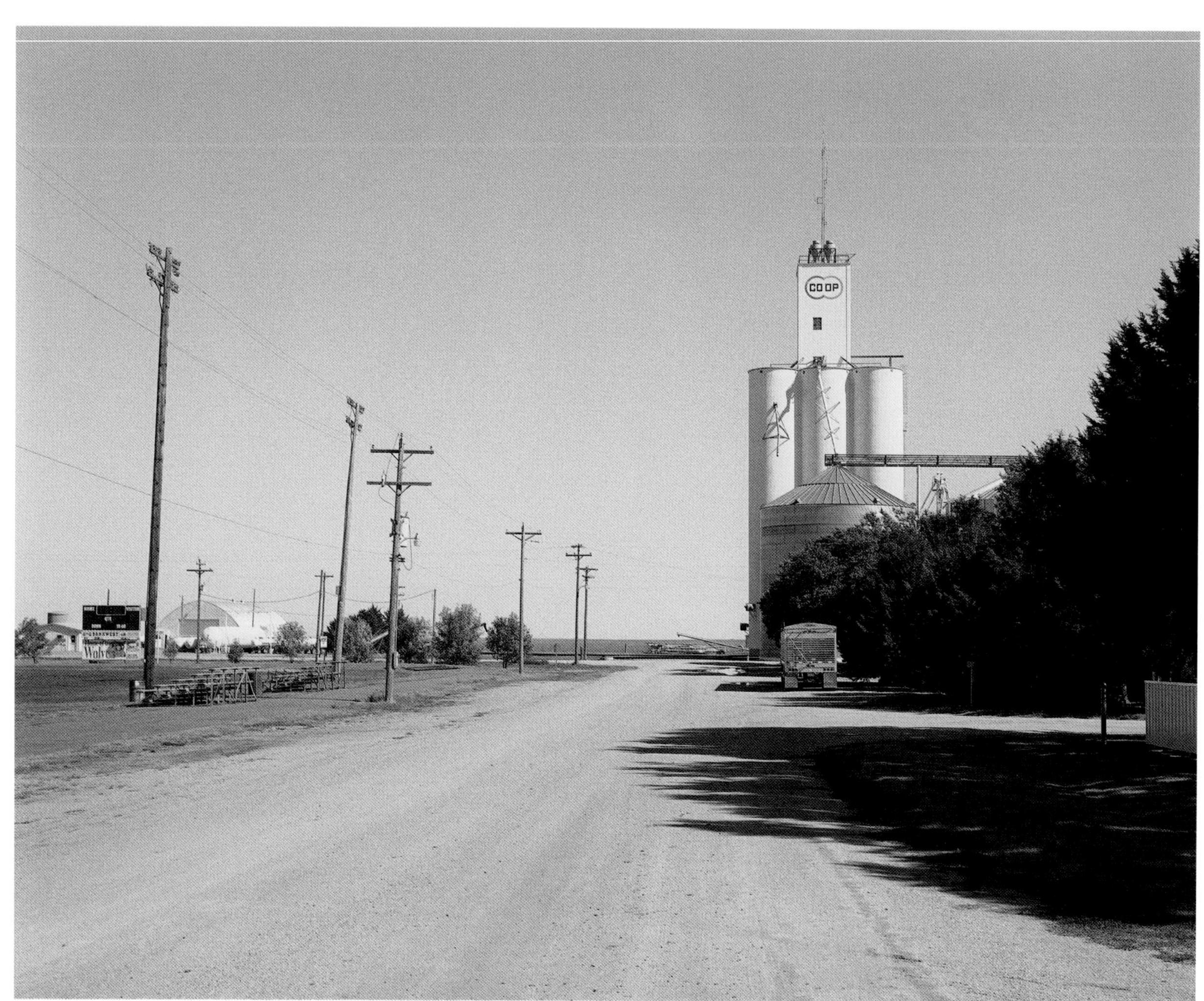
CO OP

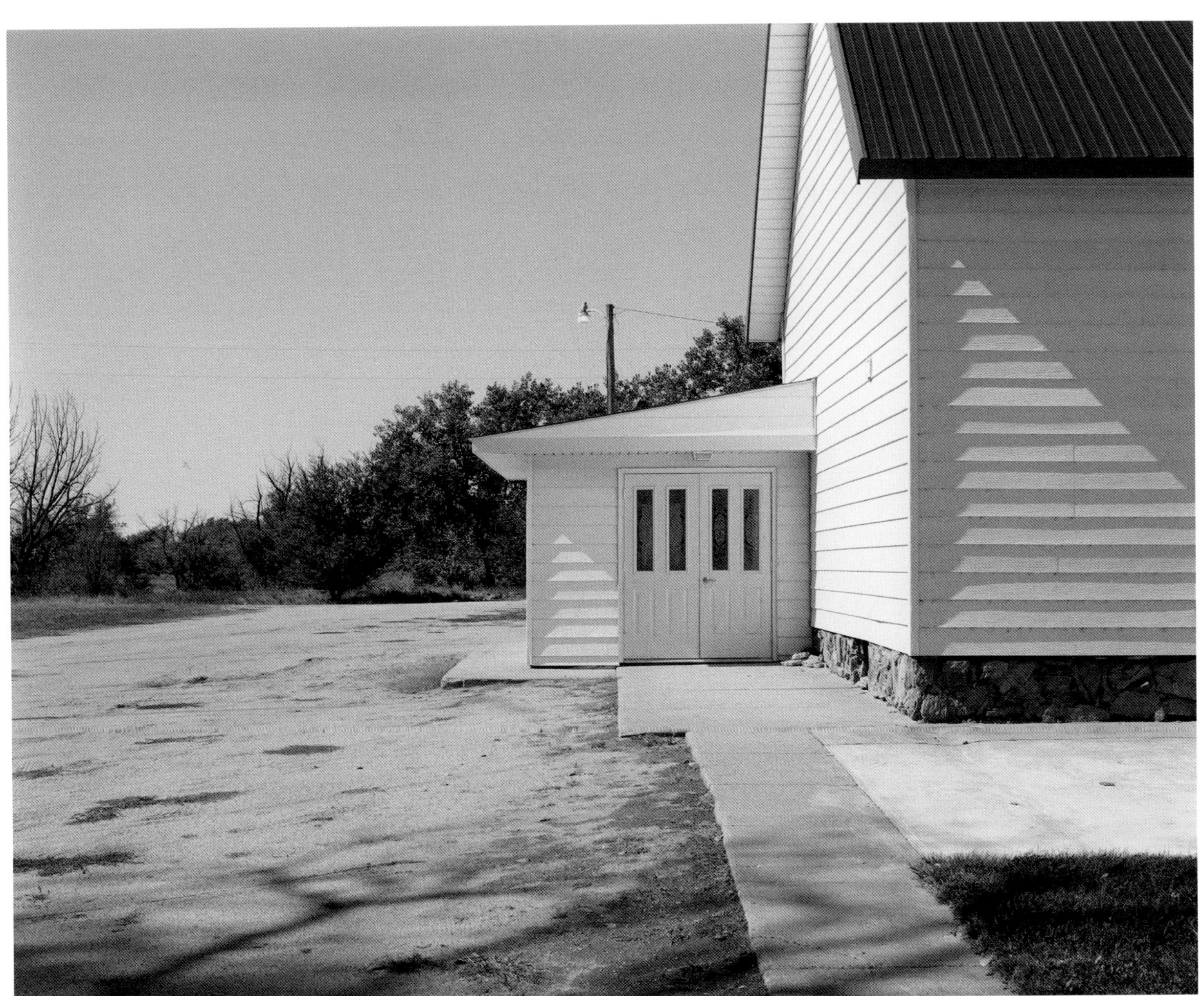

 Atwood, Kansas, Summer 2008

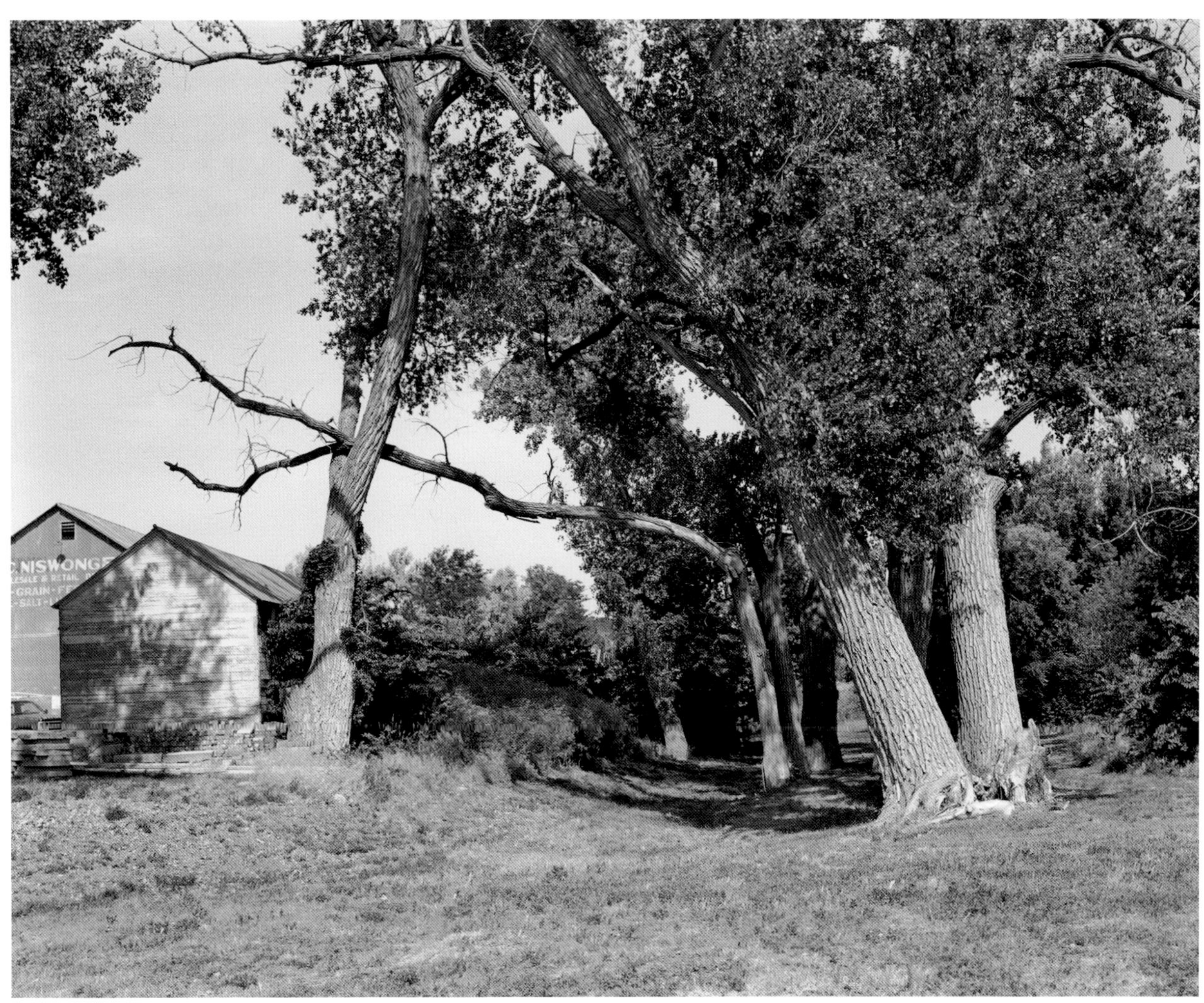
NISWONGER
WHOLESALE & RETAIL
GRAIN
SALT

29 *Near Baileyville, Kansas,* Summer 2006

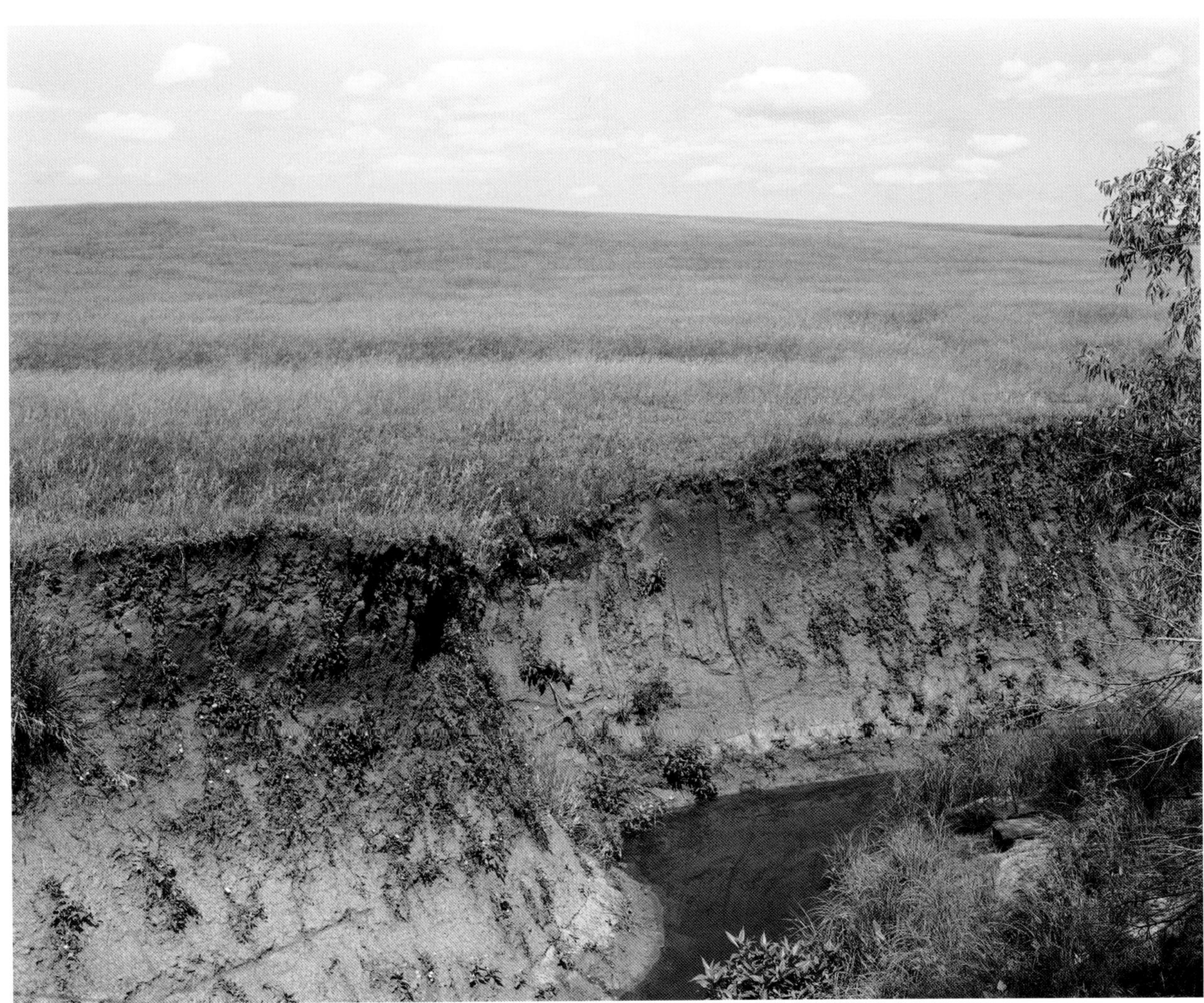

30 *Near St. Francis, Kansas,* Summer 2007

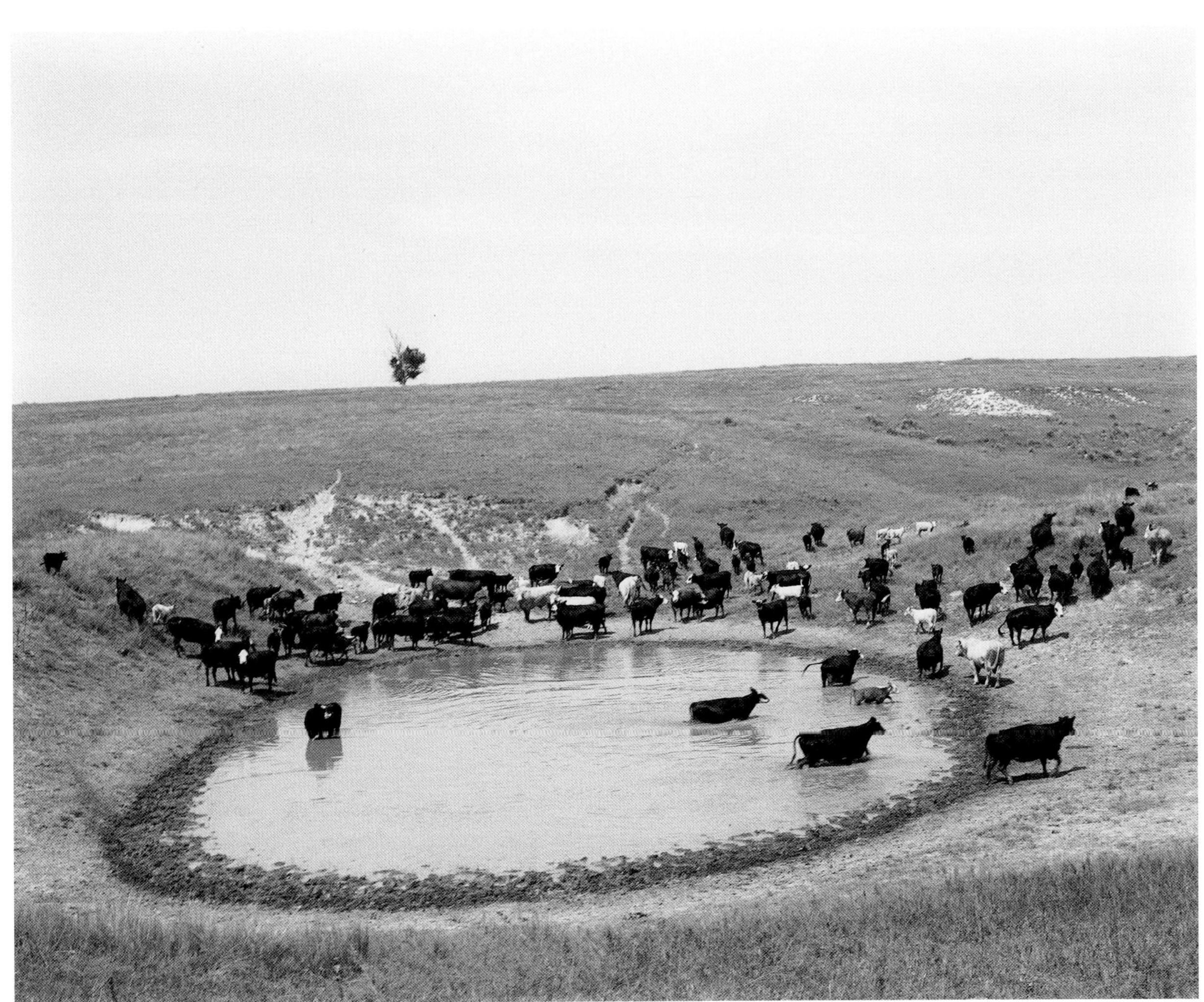

31 *Near Blakeman, Kansas,* Summer 2006

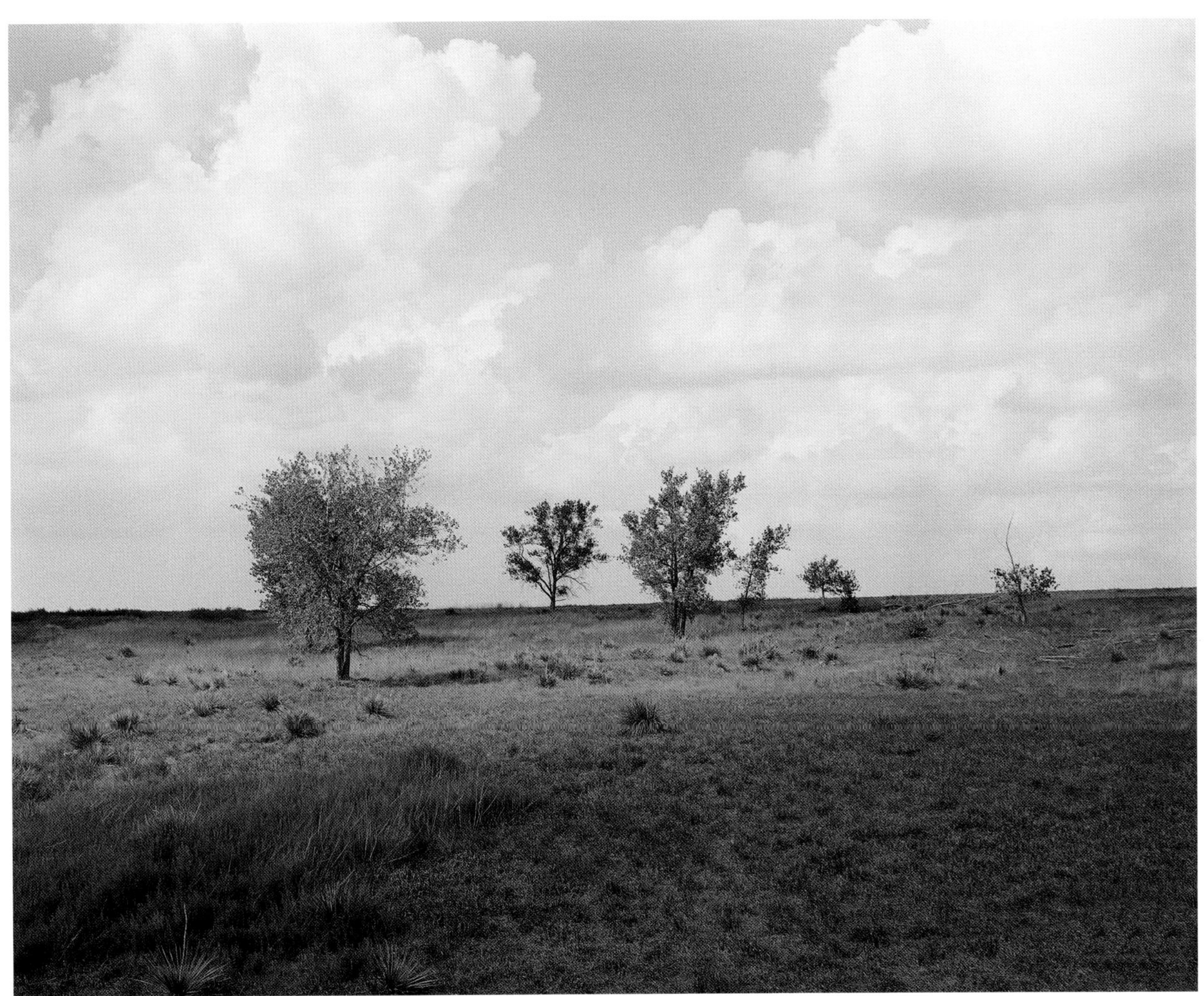

32 *Near St. Francis, Kansas,* Summer 2007

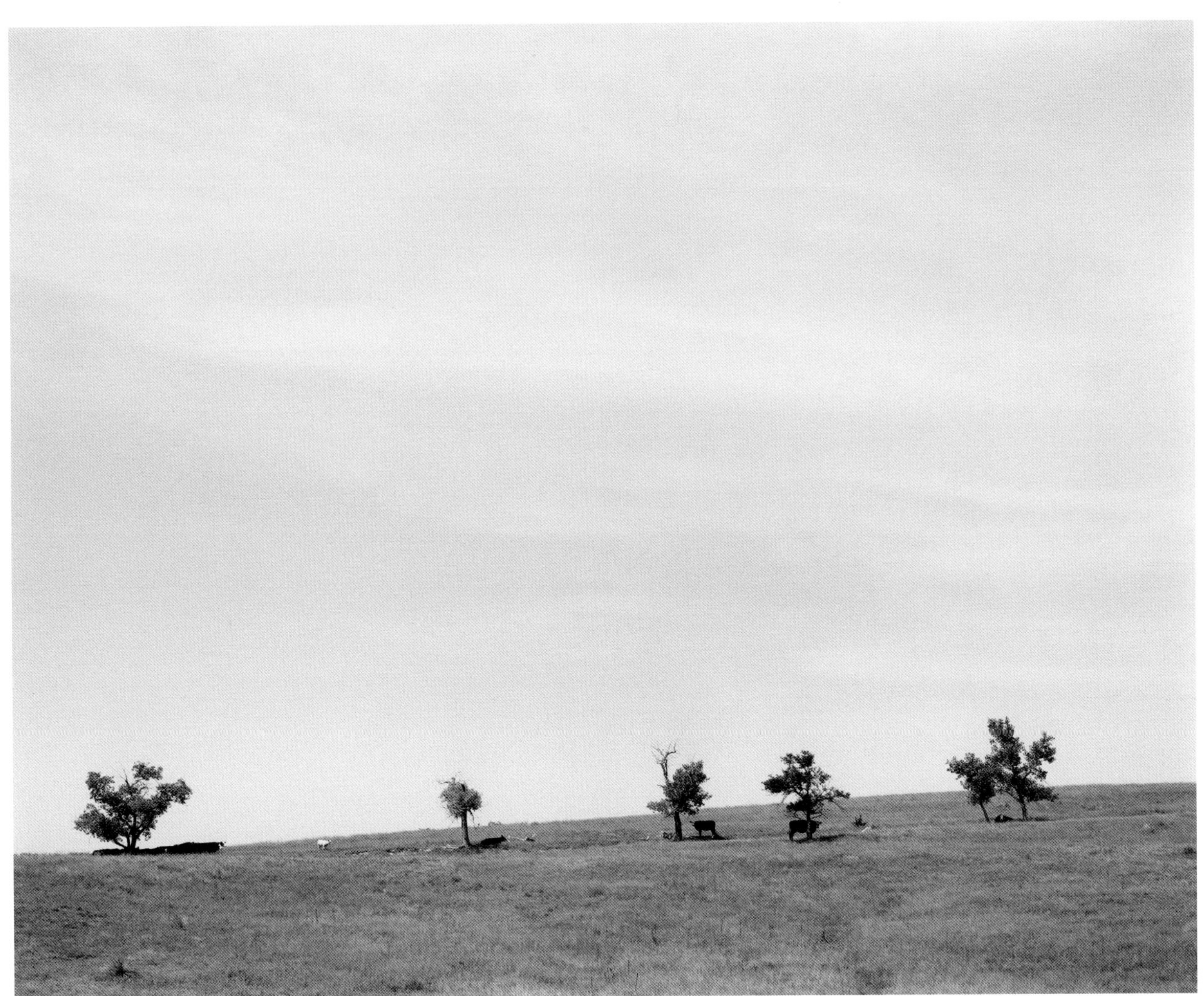

33 *Near Washington, Kansas,* Summer 2008

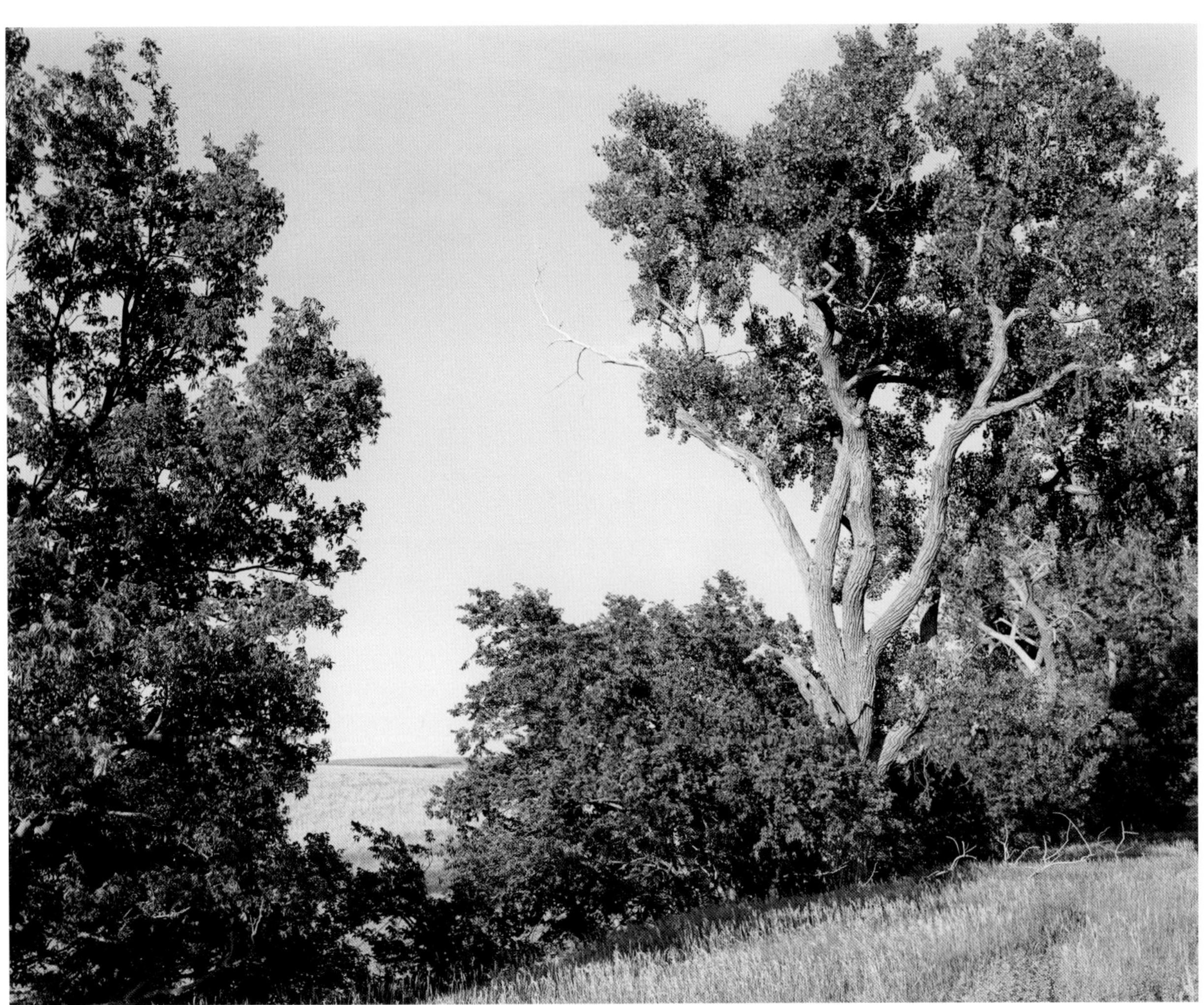

 Wheeler, Kansas, Summer 2007

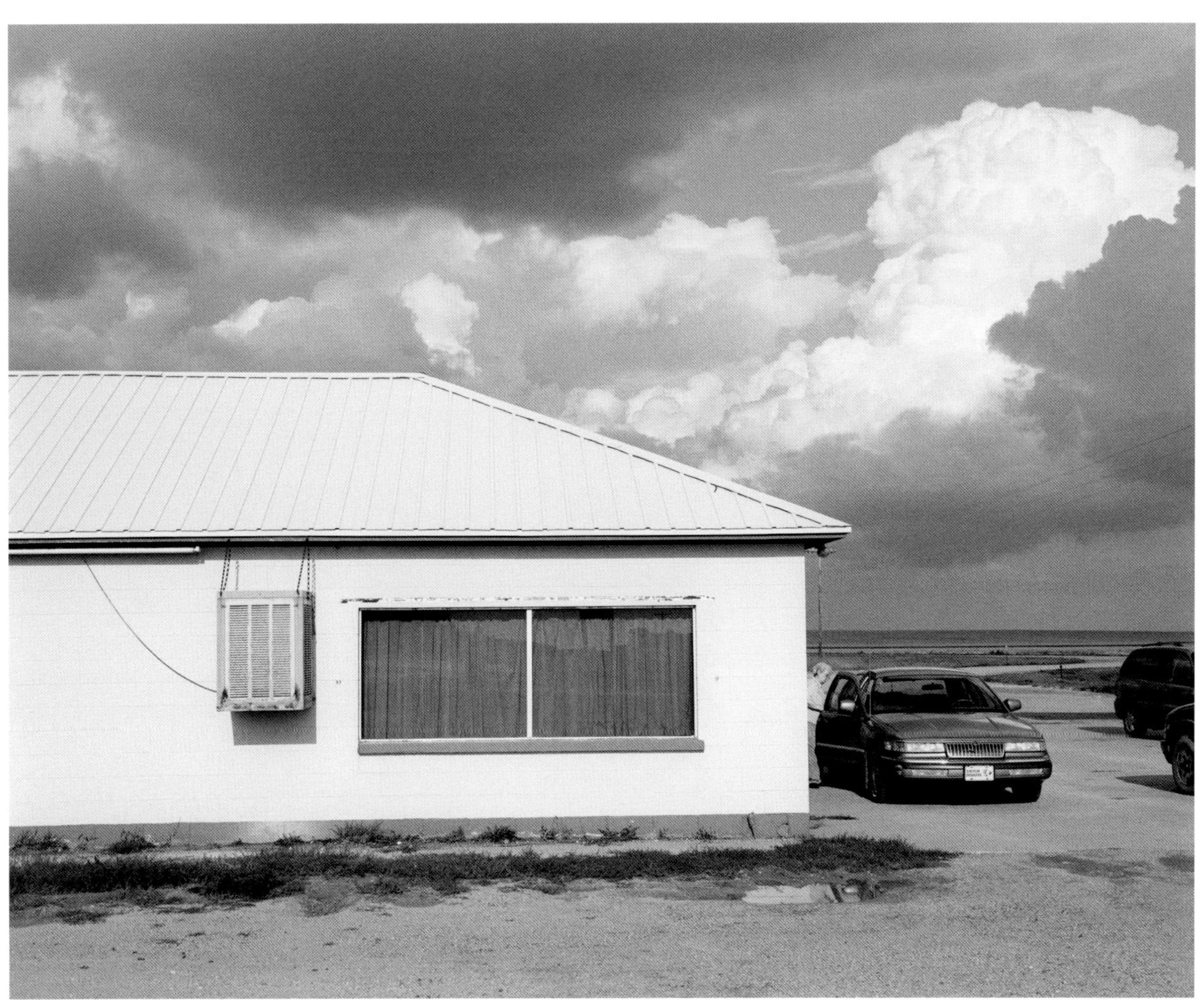

35 *St. Francis, Kansas,* Fall 2005

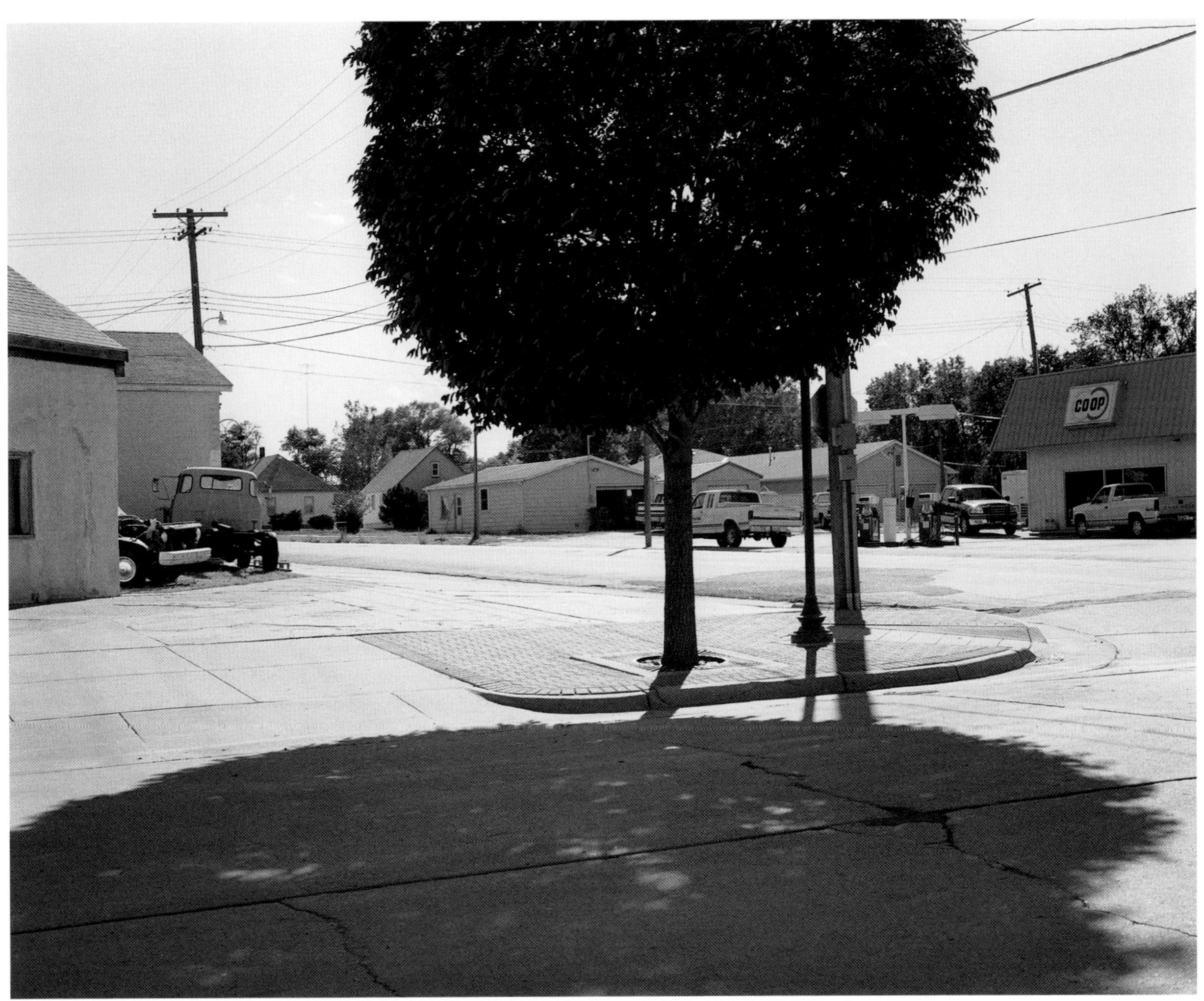

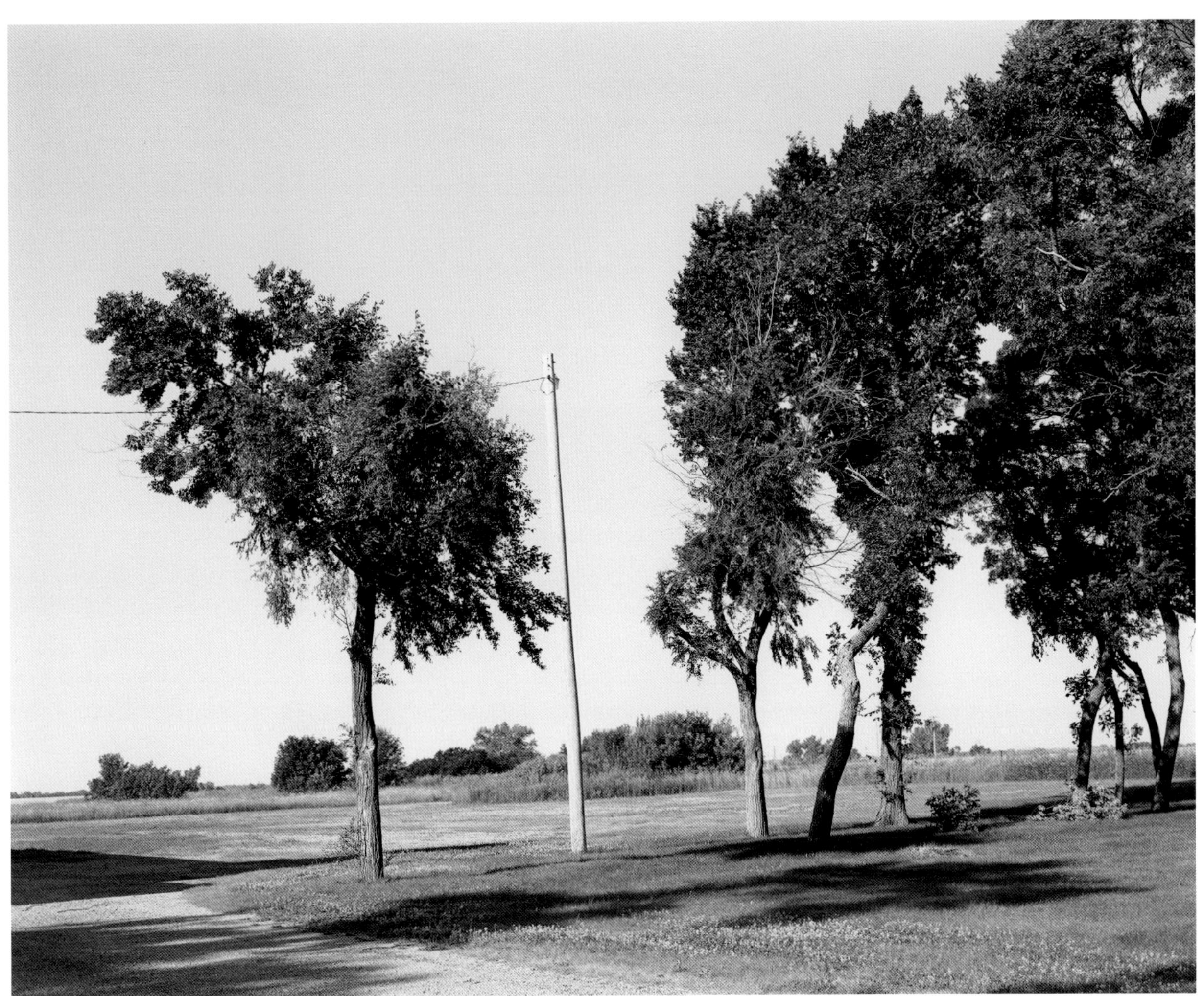

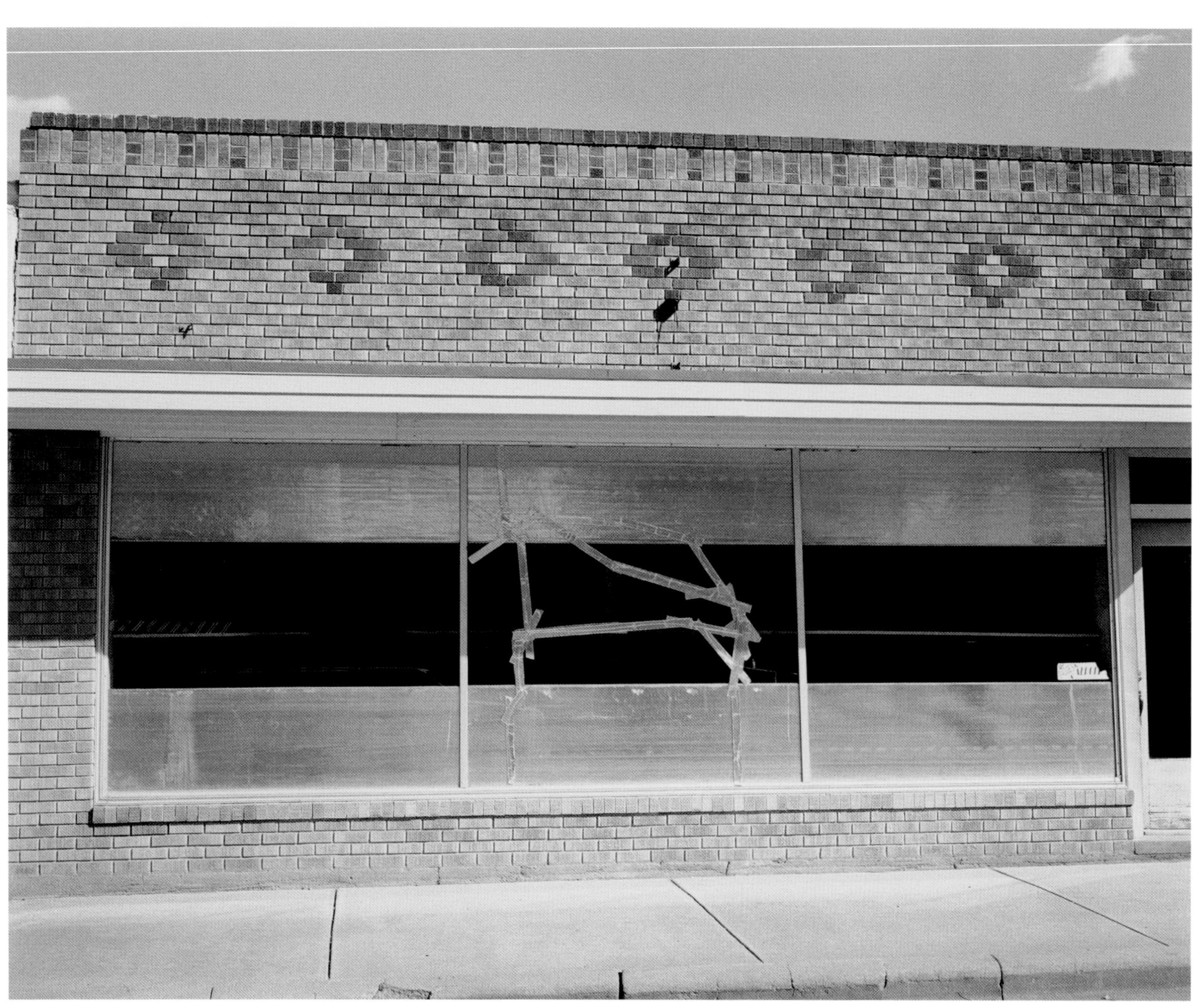

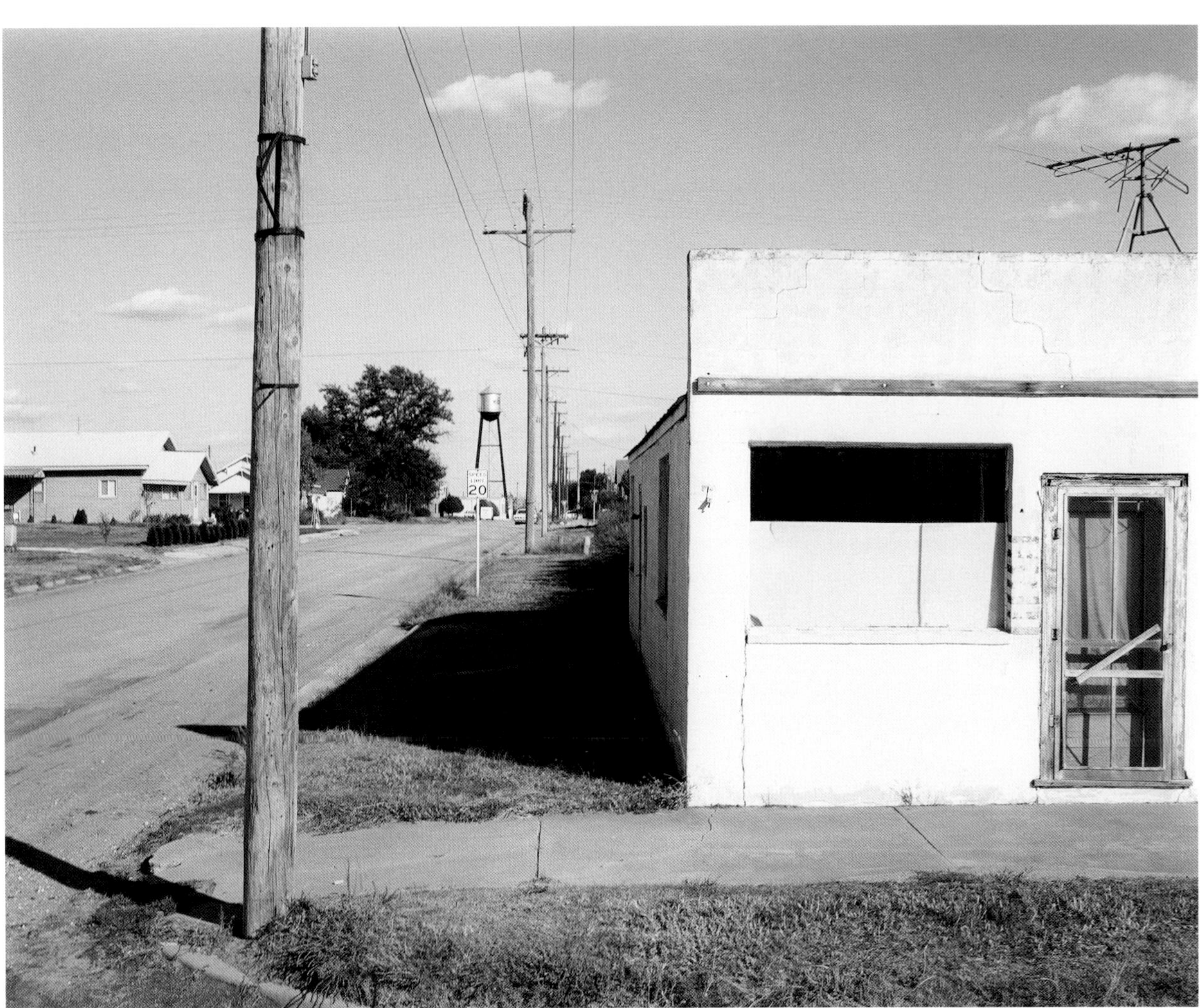

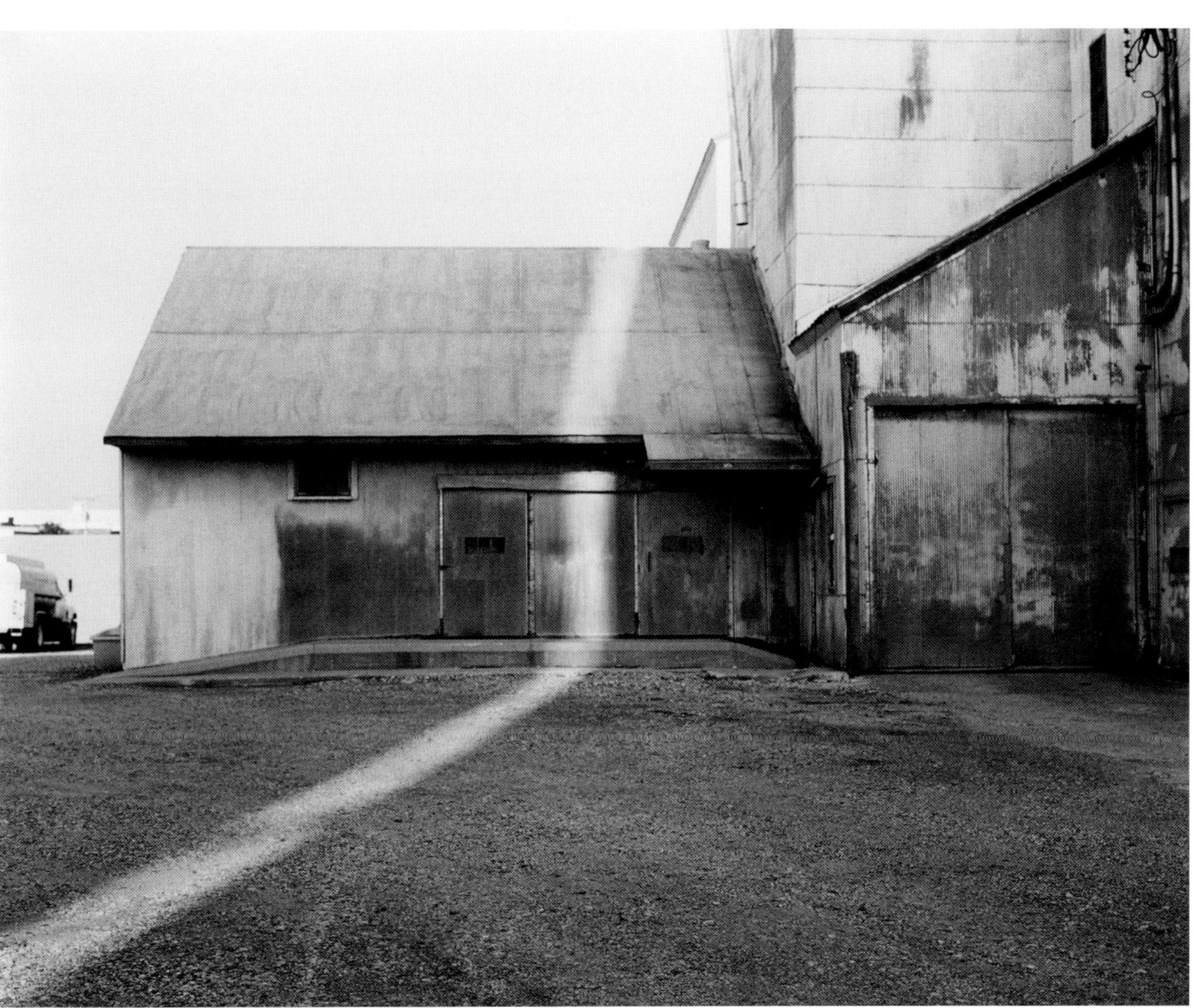

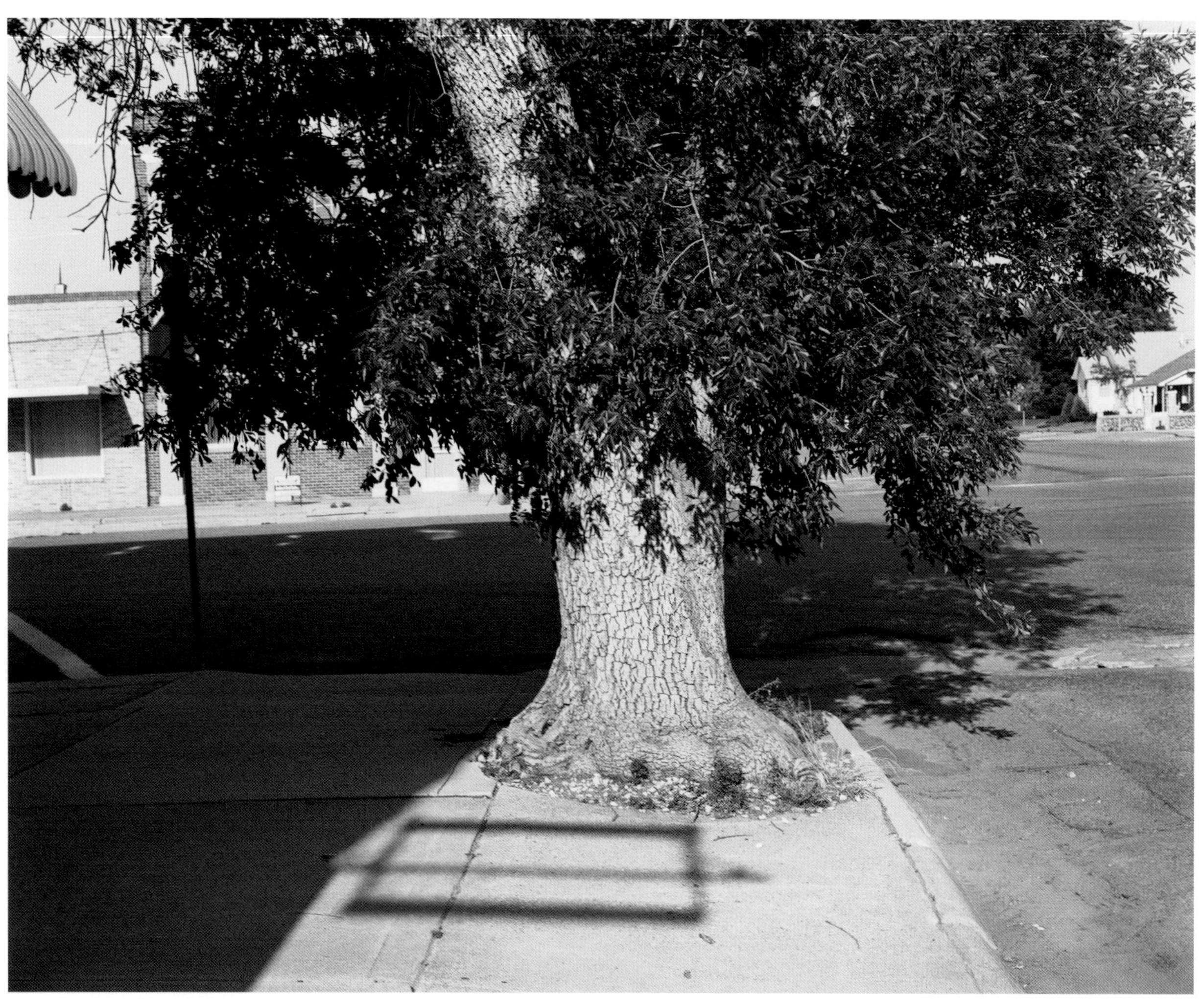

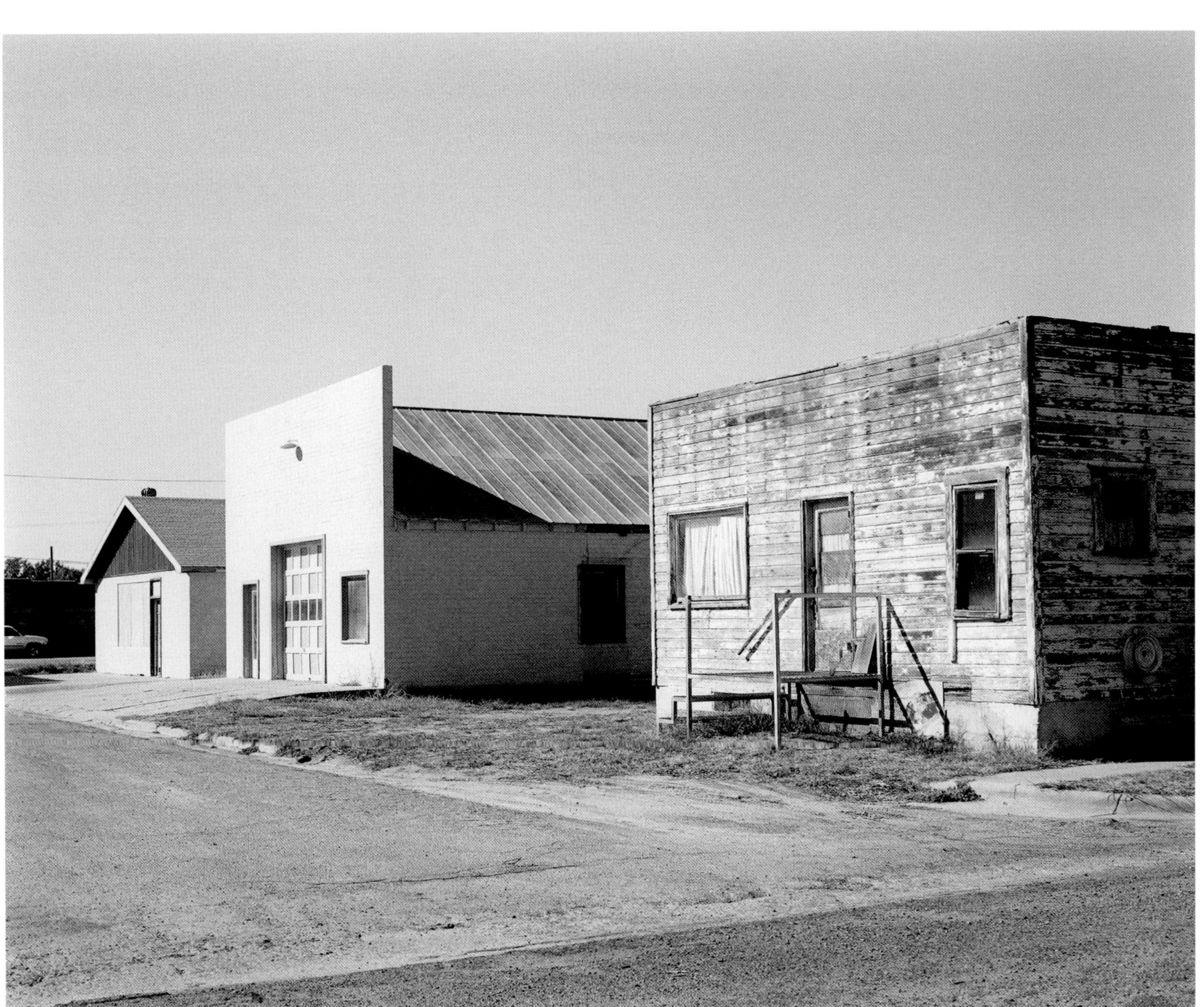

42 *Cope, Colorado,* Fall 2005

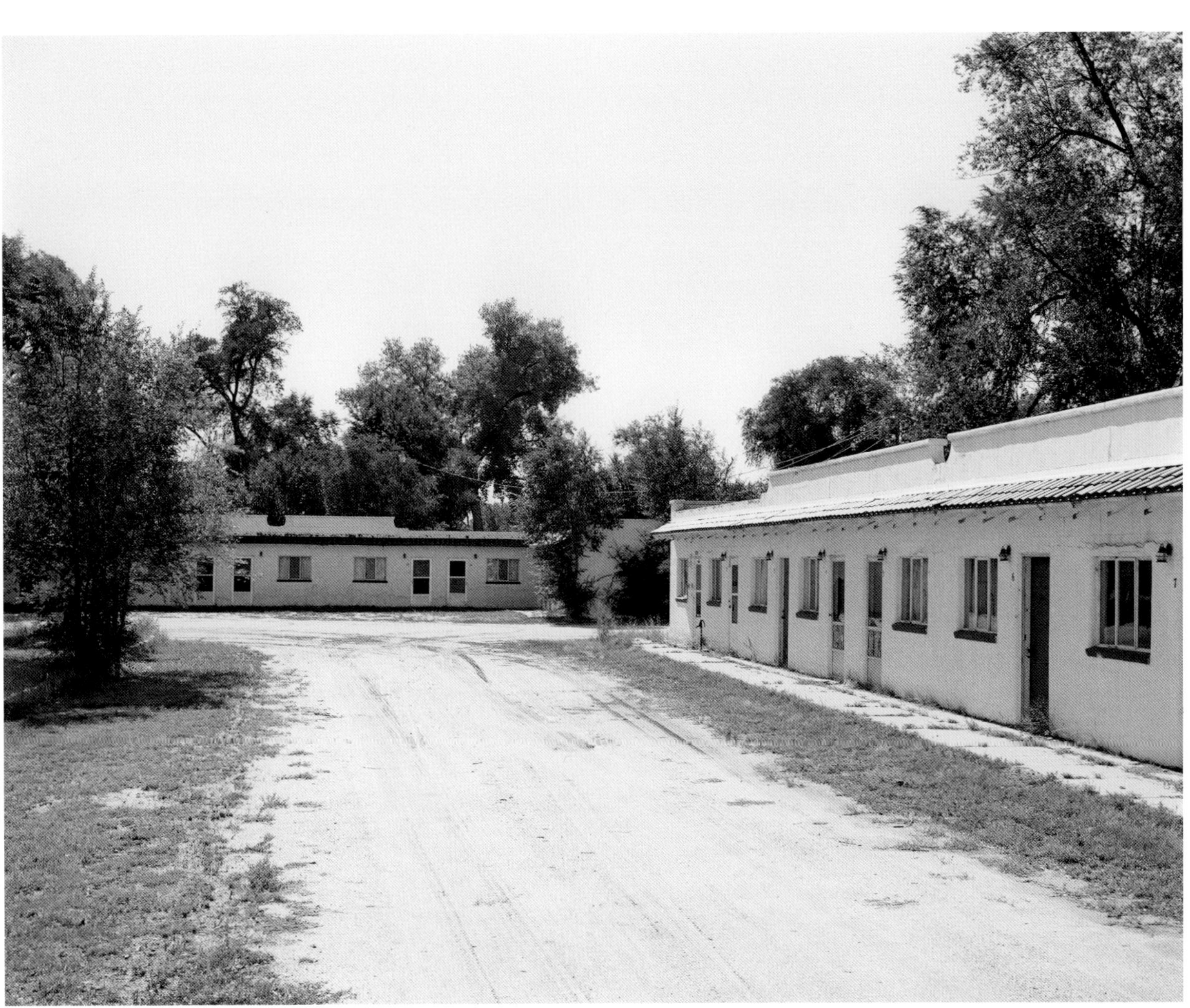

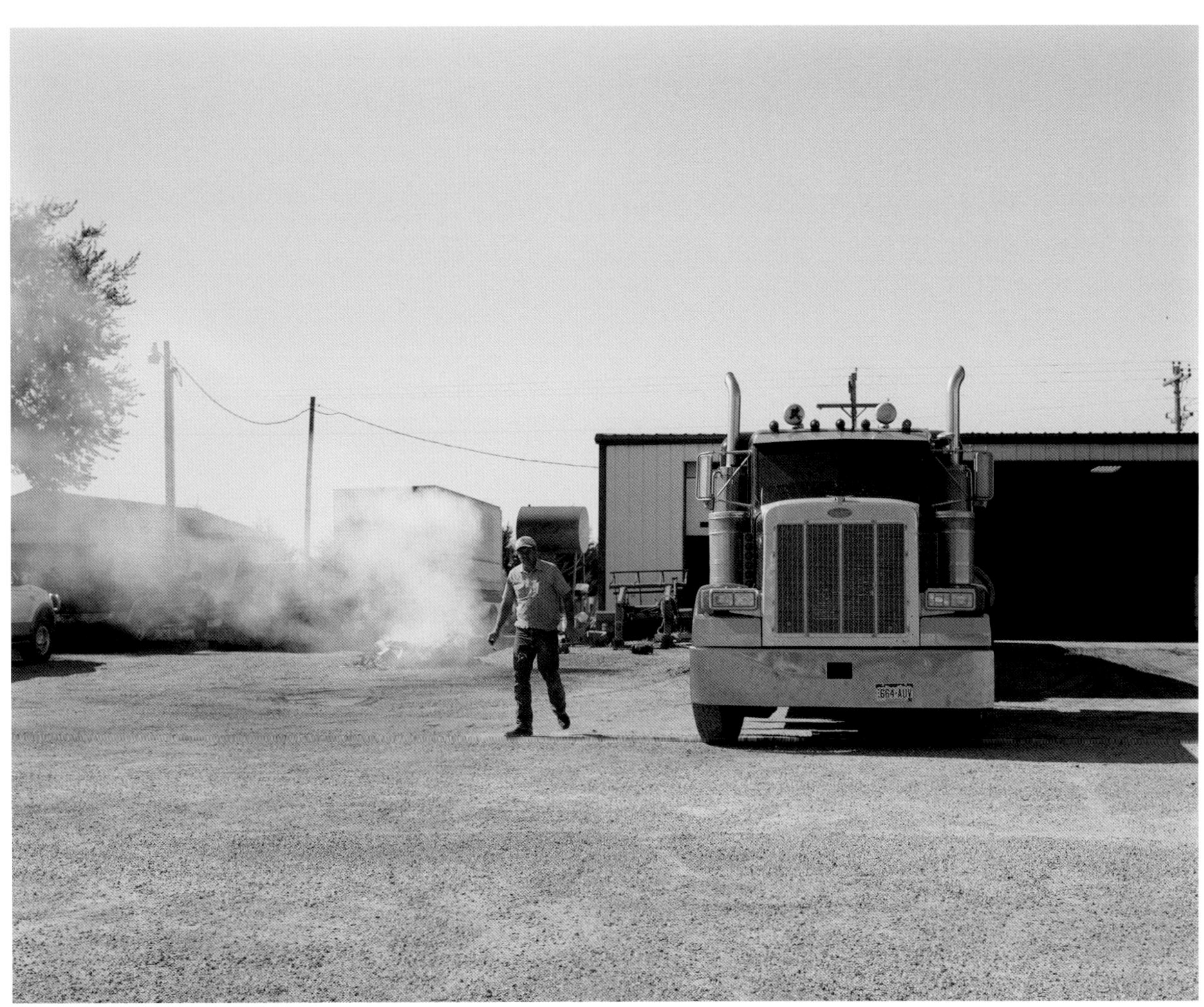

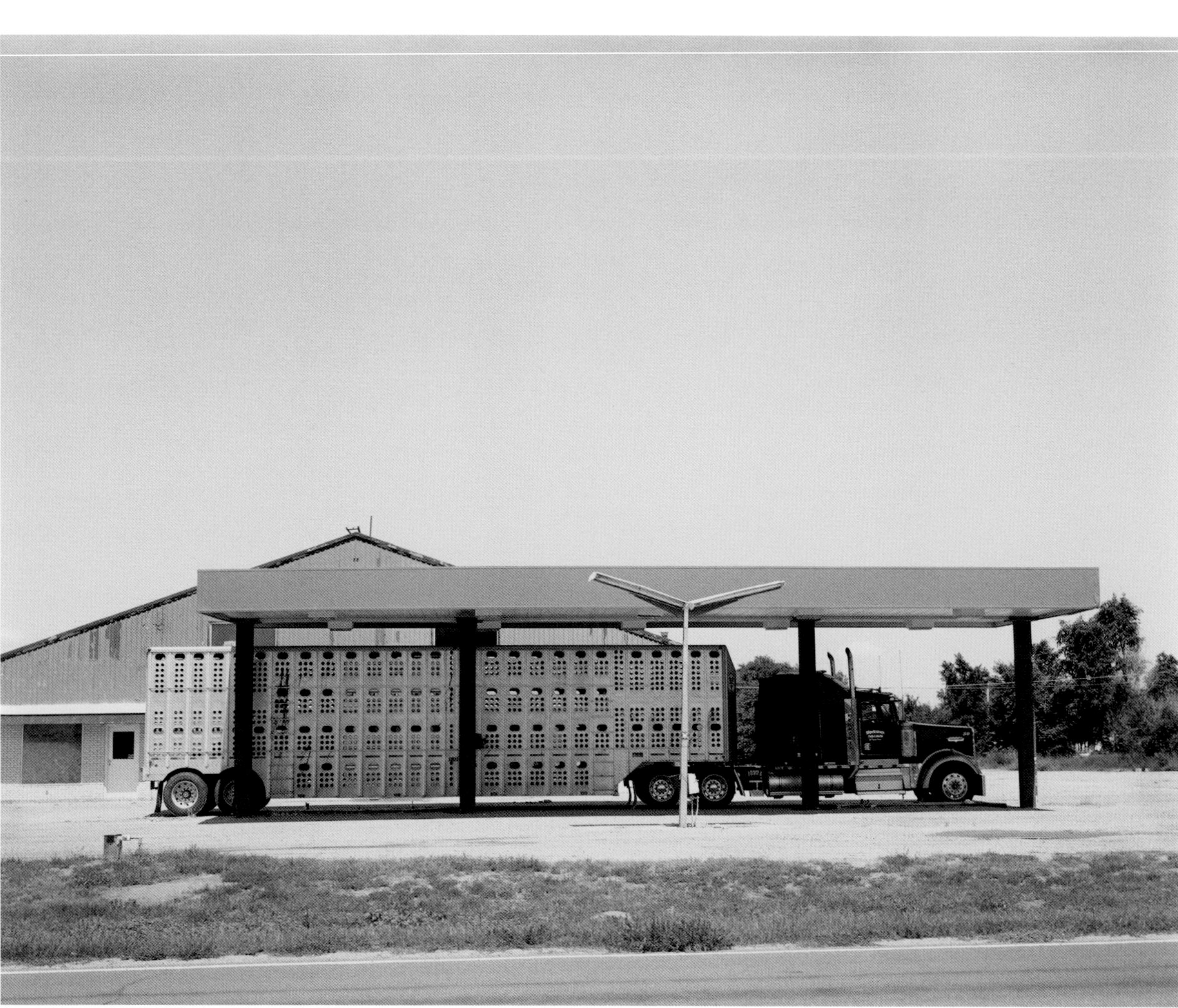

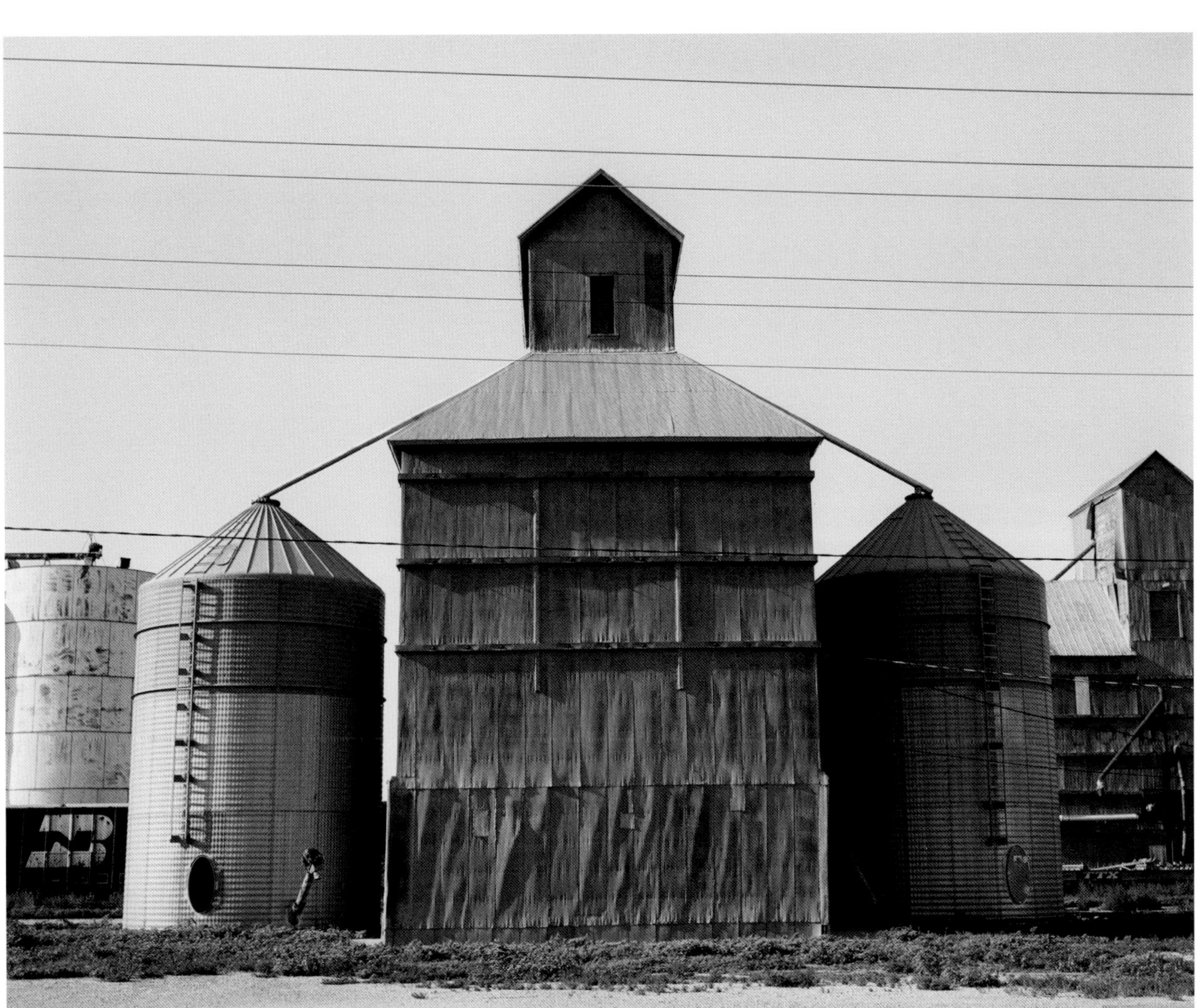

46 *Near Washington, Kansas*, Summer 2008

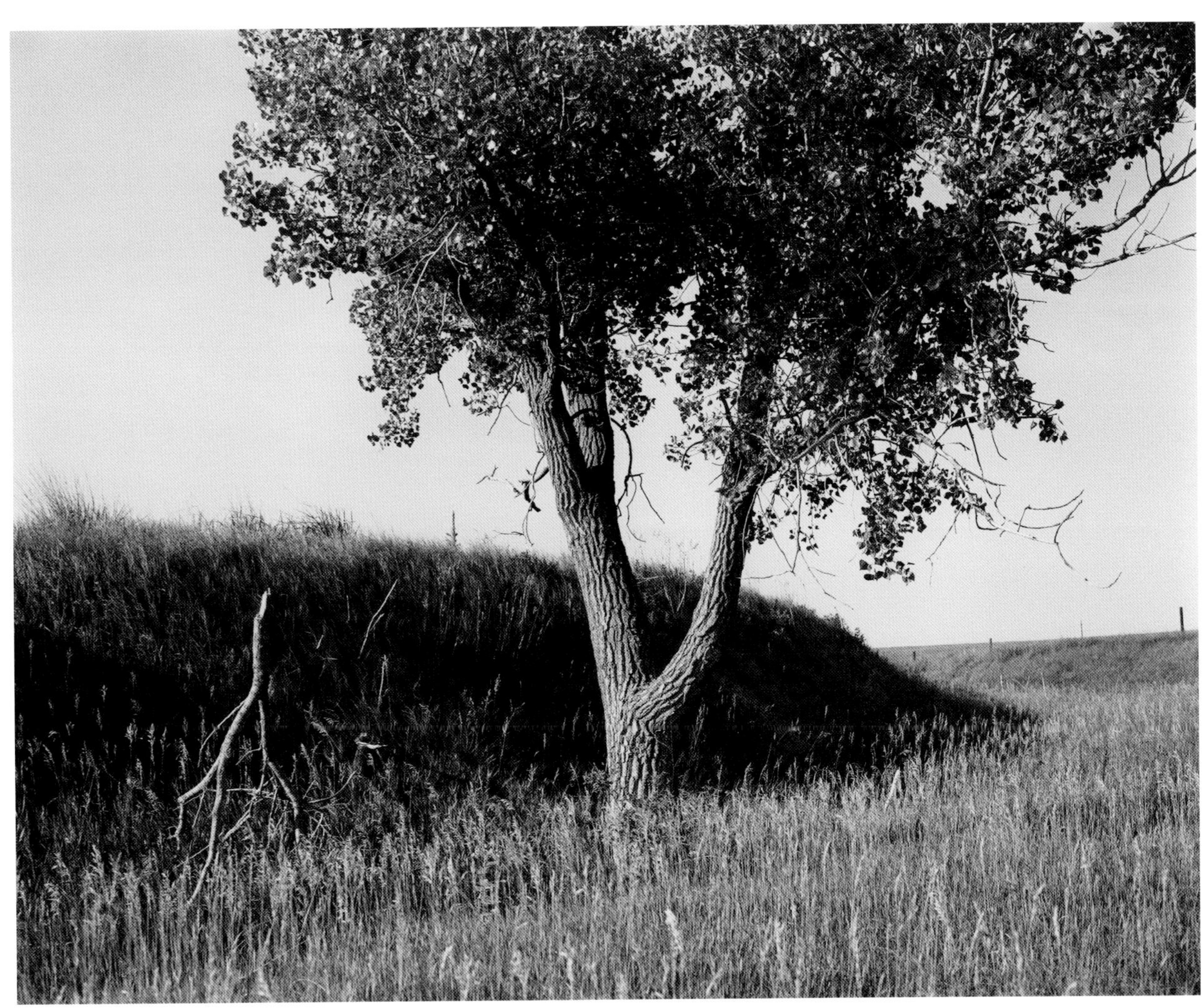

47 *Seneca, Kansas*, Summer 2007

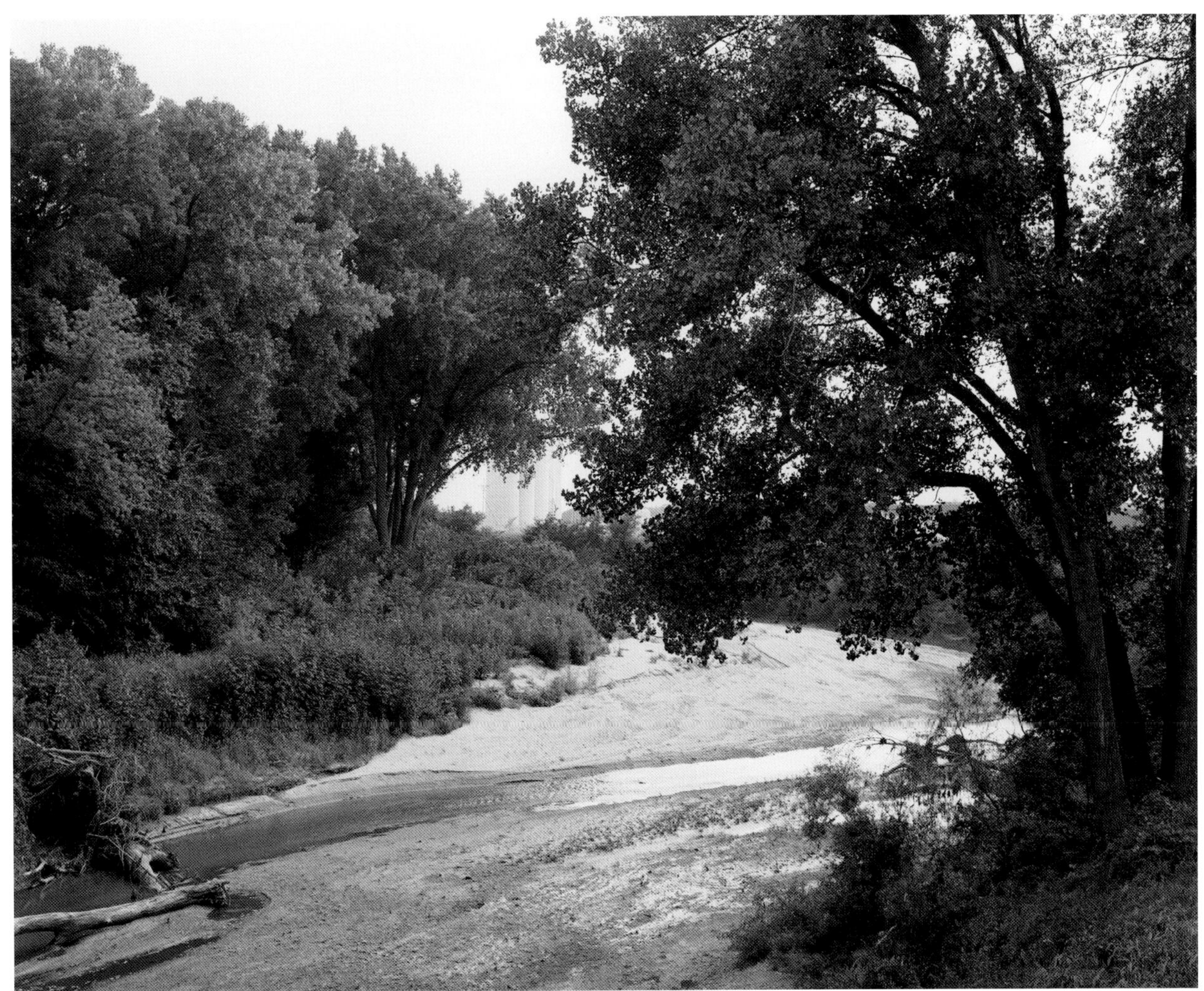

48 *Near Rydal, Kansas,* Summer 2007

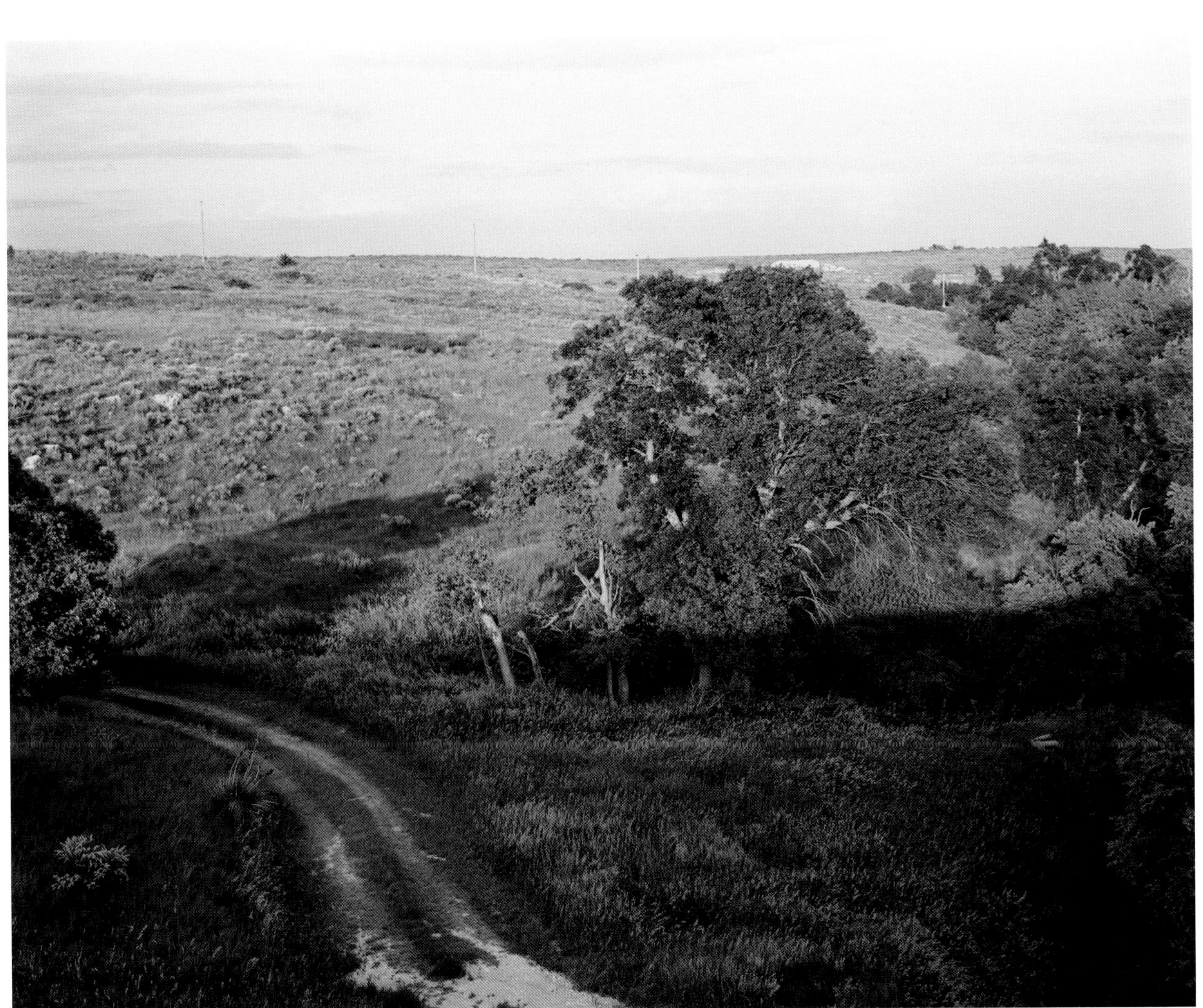

49 *Near Kanona, Kansas,* Summer 2007

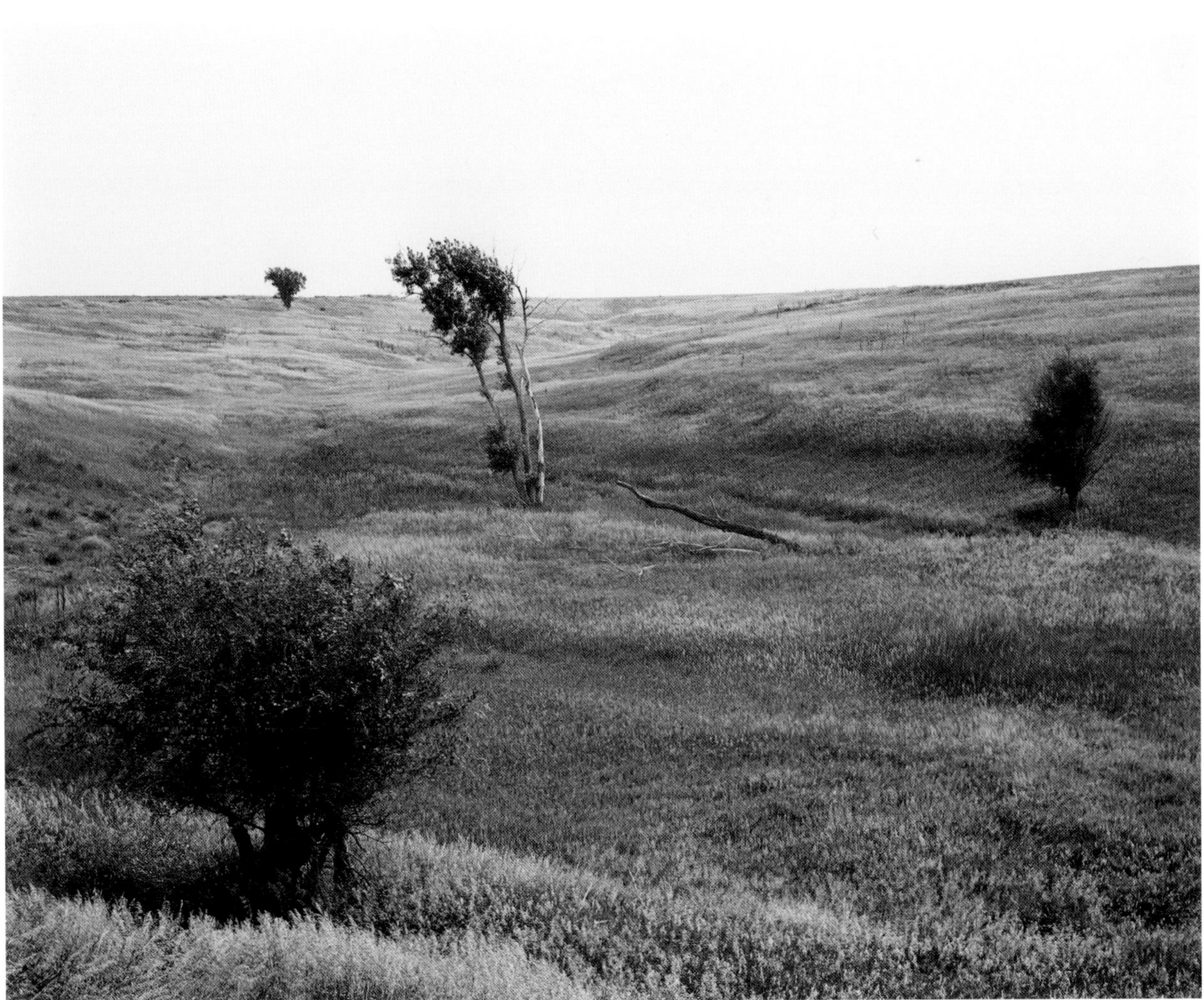

50 *Big Blue River near Marysville, Kansas*, Spring 2006

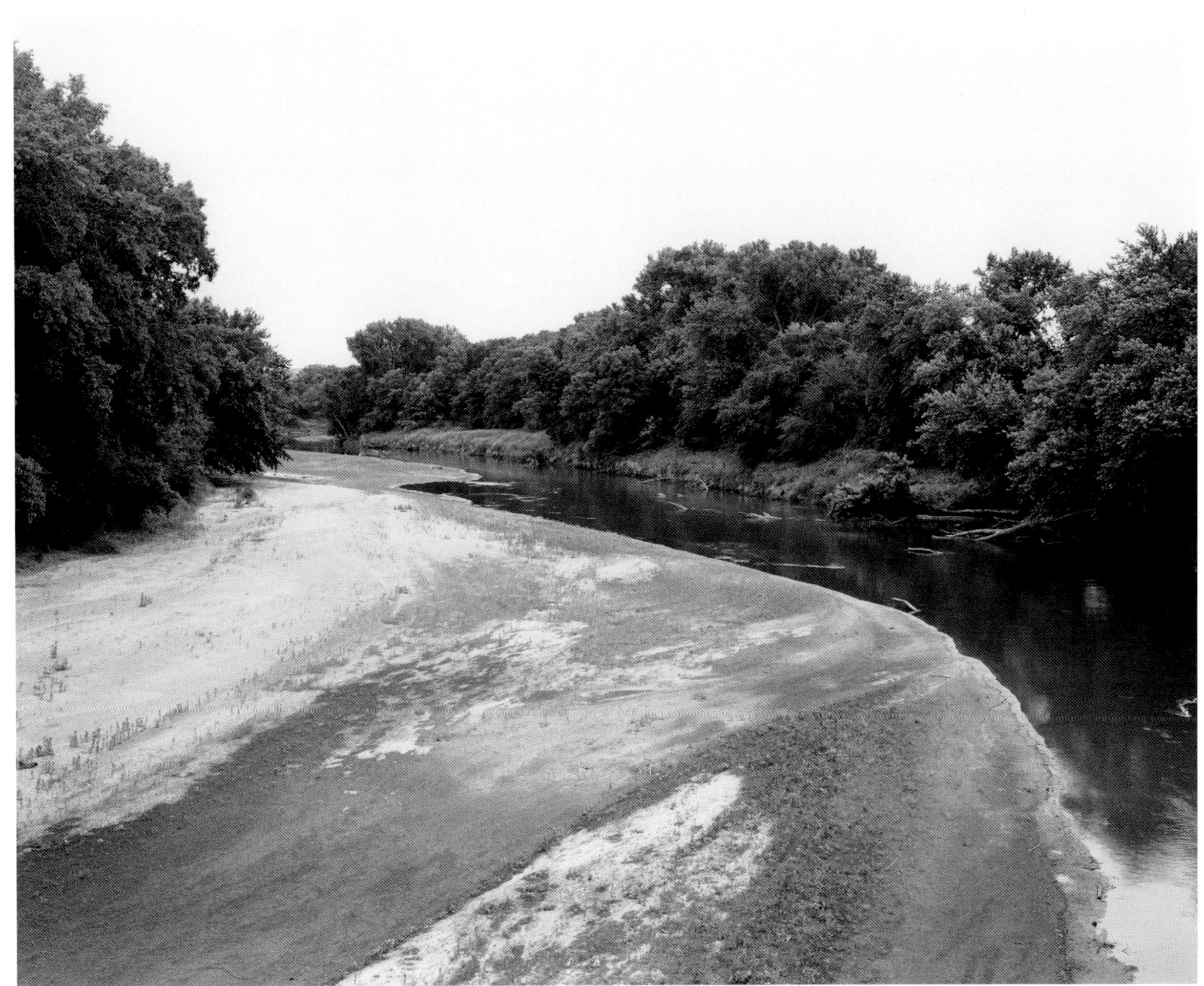

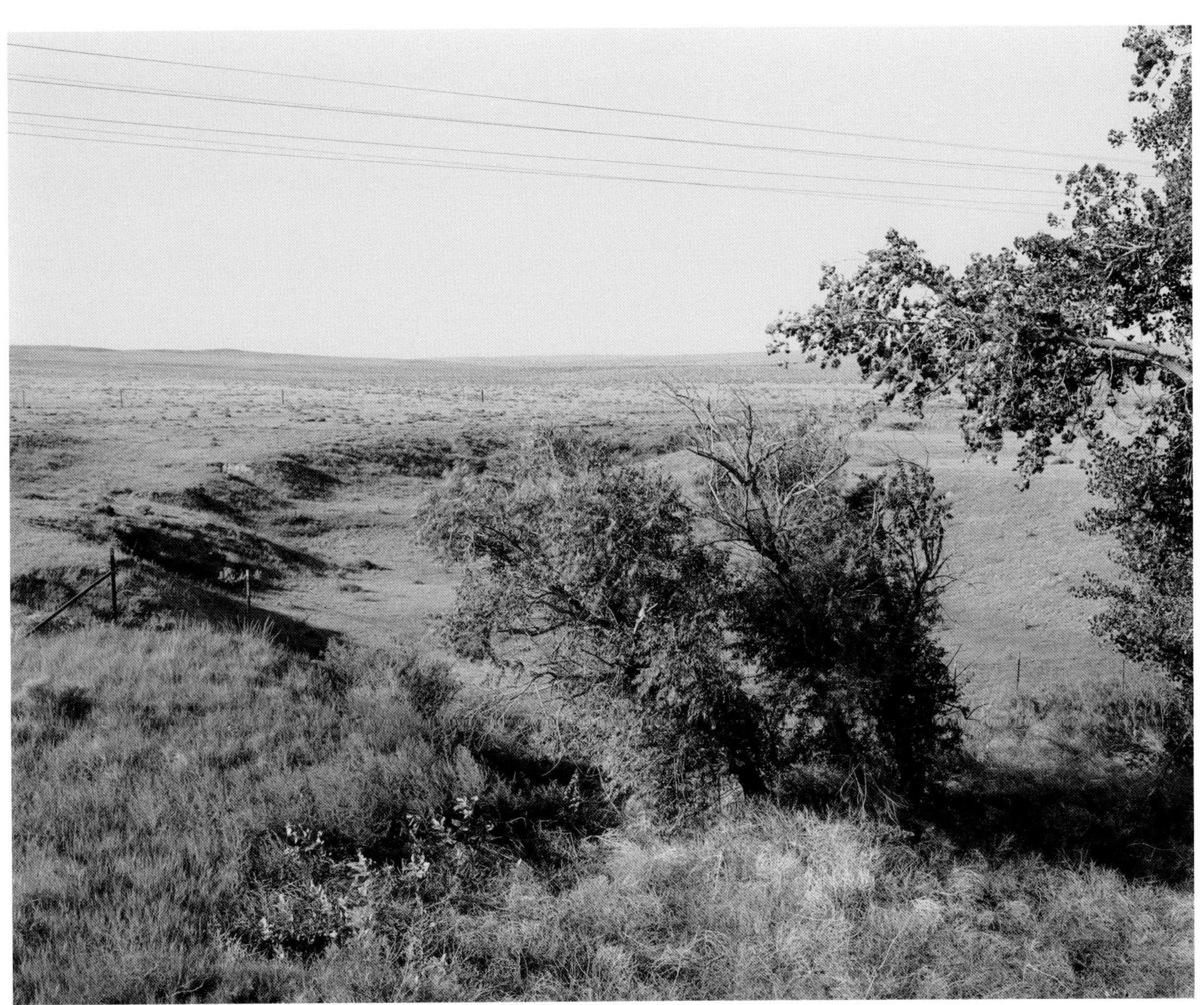

It took a long time to learn how to spell Kansas.

JOHN RYDJORD, *Indian Place Names*

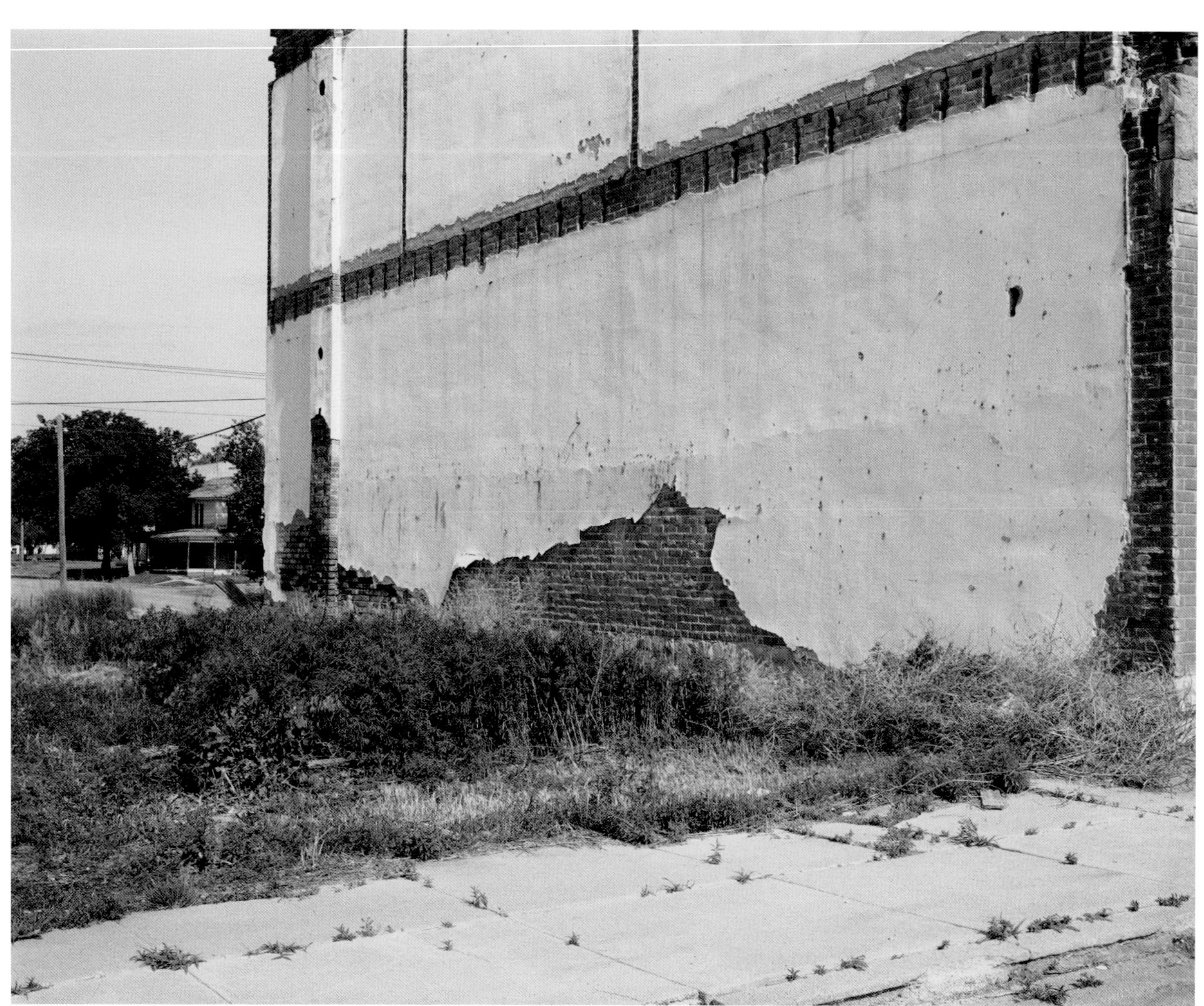

In the fall of 2005, Merrill Gilfillan suggested Route 36 as an alternative to the standard west–east Interstate-70 sameness across Kansas. Route 36 runs along the northern border of the state and offered, by his standards, a superior way to traverse that part of the country. Driving into St. Francis early next day I understood why. There was a sense of magnificence in the landscape and a generous quality to the light. I spent the next three days traveling the rest of the 375 miles across Kansas. I stopped in every town along the route to see Main Street, sample homemade café pies, and visit the silos. Back out on the highway I'd stop and walk a mile or so along each accessible creek or river. One late afternoon on Sappa Creek near Oberlin I heard the calls of migrating cranes and looked up to see hundreds of them slowly circling high overhead.

For the next four years I spent a week or so each summer migrating along Route 36 as I passed back and forth between Virginia and Colorado. The small towns and crossroads would always reveal something new, relatively speaking. Maybe a favorite building had

[FACING] *Lebanon, Kansas,* Spring 2006

been torn down, or else its empty lot would now be full of prairie flowers. A new café (serving espresso, with internet access) might have opened, or a newly renovated Deco-style movie house would be offering a feature film, but only on Saturday nights. I stopped every year near Lebanon, at the geographic center of the contiguous United States. A small park, obelisk, and defunct hotel mark the location. In homage I liked to climb up on the eight-foot-tall monument and survey the cornfields for miles around. Many towns would have music playing all day long, through speakers strung along Main Street. I recall one July day in Marysville they were playing Christmas carols while the bank sign flashed 105 degrees. With no one in sight, this felt strangely apocalyptic.

And there were the prairies, great openings where grass undulated in the breeze and cottonwood trees held down the ridges. These spaces gave a cadence to my travel and a relief from the dry desperation of the towns. While most of it was private property and fenced off, I still found plenty of access to the land where I could "get out and touch the soil" (as Wes Jackson once suggested to cross-country Kansas travelers). Walking the hills on a hot summer day, with grasshoppers flying in every direction and a thunderhead building on the horizon, my experience of time became at once more immediate and more vast. And the rare possibility of finding a rusty Gooch's Feed sign on the back of an abandoned grain silo was pure archeology to me.

My deepest gratitude goes to Merrill and to Devin Johnston. This collaboration—among Merrill, Flood, and myself—has been exciting and rewarding. Robert Adams offered encouragement, and his work has been an important influence on my own. Many others —including Corey Drieth, Edith and Emmet Gowin, Toby Jurovics, Pamela Pecchio, Adam Schreiber, George Thompson, April Watson, and Dave Woody—helped along the way. Traveling Route 36, I met a number of wonderful Kansans who enthusiastically shared their food, music, and appreciation of the prairie light. In particular, a luthier in Bird City named Dawn Petty opened her door, and minutes later I was playing a 1955 Martin guitar to accompany her on oldtime fiddle tunes. Summer research grants funded through the College of Arts and Sciences at the University of Virginia supported the making of the photographs. The generosity of Hunter and Elizabeth Lewis, Jeanne and Richard Press, and a grant from the Elizabeth Firestone Graham Foundation supported the printing of the book. Finally, Kay Jenkins nurtured this work and has always been my greatest supporter. Her love is a reassurance beyond measure.

MERRILL GILFILLAN

was born in Mount Gilead, Ohio, in 1945 and studied literature at the Universities of Michigan and Iowa. His first book of poems appeared in 1970. Recent publications include three books of poems, *Small Weathers* (Qua Books, 2004), *Undanceable* (Flood Editions, 2005), and *Selected Poems 1965–2000* (Adventures in Poetry, 2005), as well as a collection of alfresco essays, *Rivers and Birds* (Johnson Books, 2003). He currently lives in Colorado.

WILLIAM WYLIE

has published three previous books of his photographs, *Riverwalk* (University Press of Colorado, 2000), *Stillwater* (Nazraeli Press, 2002), and *Carrara* (Center for American Places, 2009), all concerned with landscape and place. He received a Guggenheim Fellowship in photography in 2005. His photographs can be found in the permanent collections of the Metropolitan Museum of Art, National Gallery of Art, Smithsonian American Art Museum, and Yale University Art Museum. He lives in Charlottesville where he teaches photography at the University of Virginia.

Published by Flood Editions

www.floodeditions.com

ISBN 978-0-9819520-3-1

Frontispiece: *Near Scandia, Kansas*, Spring 2006

Design and composition by Quemadura

Printed on acid-free, recycled paper

by Shapco Printing, Inc., Minneapolis

This book was made possible through
the generous support of Hunter and
Elizabeth Lewis, Jeanne and Richard Press,
the Elizabeth Firestone Graham Foundation,
and the Illinois Arts Council.

First Edition